Lyon's Legacy
Catalyst Chronicles: Book One

Sandra Ulbrich Almazan

2nd edition

ISBN-10:0-9838903-6-6
ISBN-13:978-0-9838903-6-2

OTHER WORKS BY THE AUTHOR

Catalyst Chronicles Series

Lyon's Legacy

Twinned Universes

Season Avatars Series

Seasons' Beginnings

Scattered Seasons

Non-Fiction

Life at Seventeen Syllables a Day: A Journal in Haiku

SF Women A-Z: A Reader's Guide

CONTENTS

ACKNOWLEDGMENTS AND DEDICATION

Thanks to Aviva Rothschild and Susan Ryan for inspiring the original draft of this story with their own works.

So many people critiqued different versions of this story that I'm not sure I remember them all. Some of the people who have helped me improve this story are Heather Barnes, Sam Butler, Susan Curnow, Heidi Garrett, Elizabeth Hull, Gregg Lipschik, Ian Morrison, Darrell Newton, Walter Williams, Ann Winter, and Zvi Zaks. With the exception of Heather Barnes, they were or are members of the Online Writing Workshop for SF, Fantasy, and Horror. If I've missed anyone, I apologize. Any errors in this book are my own.

Lauren Sweet was both developmental editor and copyeditor, and Meghan Derico of Derico Photography designed the cover. Both of them did fantastic jobs.

Special thanks go out to my husband, Eugene Almazan, and my son, Alex, for supporting me through the writing and publishing process.

I would like to dedicate this novella to my writing mentor, Kathleen Massie-Ferch, who passed away in 2002.

PROLOGUE

I know this must be very upsetting for you. You weren't expecting this at all. I don't blame you if you're furious. But before you say you hate me forever, please understand I did what I thought was best for you. I don't have any idea what it's like being you, but I've been through something similar. At least listen to my story before you storm off and shut the door....

CHAPTER ONE

People always call when you're in the middle of something uninterruptable, like sampling kidneys. My elbow-length gloves were immersed in ripe-smelling nutrient broth as I cornered the Brooks-Jones kidney in the tank, trying not to squeeze it. Just when I had it, my handheld chimed in the pocket of my lab coat. My hands slipped, and the half-grown kidney darted off. As much as I wanted to drop the handheld in the broth, I didn't dare; the chime pattern indicated someone from company headquarters was calling. And that meant it was time for my least favorite job.

I lifted one hand out of the broth and shook it off before answering, still chasing the errant kidney with the other hand. "Jo here."

"This is Catherine." The company president's personal assistant—my hunch was right. "Are you busy?"

I reached back into the tank and grasped the squishy organ. "I'm in the middle of sampling."

"Is there another tech out there who can take over?"

There were three, but they were more interested in gossiping than taking care of the organs. I sampled some cells from the kidney with a syringe and injected them into the auto-analyzer. As I waited for results, I asked, "Does Mr. Guzman want to show me off to another set of clients?"

I never liked being on display. Even people who didn't know anything about TwenCen music recognized me, thanks to all the ads featuring my superstar great-grandparents, Sean and Baby Lyon. My face is the female version of Sean's. Every time Guzman showed me off, he made it sound as if Golden Helix had sculpted my features. I don't know why he did that; Golden Helix grows organs for transplants. It has nothing to do with gene sculpting. Besides, I came by my great-granddad's face naturally, through my dad.

Lucky me.

Silence. Then Catherine said, "Yes, but it's not what you're thinking. Your name has been brought up for an important assignment. I think it would pay a considerable bonus."

A bonus! The magic word, even better than "please." Mom's medicines and the board at the TransAIDS Long-Term Care Clinic had consumed all our savings. A bonus would make it easier for me to return to grad school and genetics.

The auto-analyzer bleeped; the kidney was developing within specs. I took that as a good omen. "So, when's the meeting?"

"They're just waiting for one more person."

Typical; wait till the last minute to tell me what's going on. The latex gloves snapped as I pulled them off. "I'll be there in five minutes." I disconnected before Catherine could add anything else. I tilted my cap so the brim shadowed my face, took off my lab coat, shoved my handheld into its slot on my belt, and headed up to the main office.

* * *

I was the only one in the vator on my way to the twentieth floor, but even here, I couldn't find peace. A smartad of white-skinned teenage girls romping in a virtual meadow materialized in front of my eyes. Accompanying it was an ineptly synthesized but still recognizable song: "Knowing." The kids were out of tune, and the lead singer—a blonde with huge, sculpted breasts—couldn't keep the beat if you handed it to her in a bag. I was probably the only one in the world who noticed, though, or even cared. The important thing was that the group was sexy enough to get horny fourteen-year-olds to download their cover of my great-granddad's song. Another number one for them, and another hundred grand for my cousins. I chopped my hand through the smartad and was satisfied by the resulting silence.

Before another one could start, the doors opened onto Golden Helix's reception room. Sitting across from me was a fiftyish woman in a hot pink blazer and turquoise jeans. Silver earrings with pink and blue stones dangled from one ear, matching the stud in her nose. She was bent over her handheld like any other businesswoman, but over the years, I've learned to detect a fan at fifty paces. Unfortunately, she must have sensed me at the same time. She looked up, and awe shone in her eyes. "The face that launched a revolution!" she quoted at me as she stood up.

I've always hated that line from Sean's biography. Sean had inspired the Filipinos to revolt against the Marcos regime with his music and actions, not his looks. But if this woman knew the line, then she had to be the person I was supposed to meet.

I put on my fan smile. Holding out my hand (and hoping she didn't kiss it) I said the ritual words, "Hi. I'm Joanna Lyon, Sean Lyon's great-granddaughter."

"Zoë Clairdon, Music Historian for World Music." Her long pink nails bit my skin, and she held my hand too long. But this was an "I-can't-believe-I'm-touching-Sean's-descendant!" handshake, so I let it slide. "Ms. Lyon, this is such an honor!" She peered at me. "It's quite uncanny, the way you look so much like Sean after all this time."

"I'm a strand off the ol' DNA."

My remark must not have matched her expectations of Lyon humor, for she continued, "I was a teenager when I came across a holo about Sean, and it changed my life! It inspired me to study music history."

She continued her chatter while I led us to the big conference room. Guzman, the company president, was already there, talking with half a dozen other people, some in formal suits and designer jeans, others in casual clothing that had half a dozen tech apps woven into the fabric.

Guzman beckoned me over. He surprised me by not trumpeting my pedigree to the skies. Instead, he simply said, "And this is Joanna Lyon, the one who will ultimately decide the success of this project."

I was so puzzled—and a little flattered—by that remark that I missed most of the people's names. I did catch a few titles. Some of the casually dressed people were physicists; the suits were from World Music. Before I could figure out what that meant, I saw a face I knew. Plastic surgery to remove his wrinkles and sagging jowls had left intact the sharp cheekbones and straight nose we both shared.

"Uncle Jack—" I stopped myself from blurting out the rest of my private nickname for him—Uncle Jackass. He was the heir to Sean's well of dreams—not to mention the money well. What was he doing here?

"Hello, Jo" He smiled, but his eyes showed me nothing but contempt. "How's your mother?"

As if he cared. "She's gained a little weight since the doctor prescribed pot brownies, but her white blood cells are still rarer than gays in the Fundie party. The closest I can get to her is the other side of the Plexiglas wall. Course, I can't hug her without bruising her anyway—or getting TransAIDS myself." Stretching to my full height, I stepped closer and looked him in the eye. "When are you going to make that donation to the TransAIDS Foundation? You said you would!"

He scowled and turned his back to me.

I didn't know why they wanted two Lyons at a Golden Helix meeting, but I doubted it was to sing. I grabbed a cup of hazelnut coffee and sat next to Zoë, as far away from my uncle as I could.

* * *

Forty minutes later, I wished I hadn't drunk so much coffee. I was used to safety meetings that ended after half an hour, but this meeting had barely begun. All the suits from World Music had done was show us an interminable number of graphs about their poor profits. I wondered if Guzman cared any more than I did. I crossed my legs under the table and hoped my bladder wouldn't burst. You'd think I'd get organ cloning as a benefit, but Golden Helix wasn't that generous.

"Of course, some historical artists have always sold steadily, and if their current sales don't match up to the hottest current artists, their cumulative sales are far more impressive," one of the suits said. "I'm not just talking about Elvis Presley, but also Bob Dylan, The Who, The Rolling Stones, Jimi Hendrix—rock'n'roll legends may die, gentles, but their sales only get better."

I noticed he hadn't mentioned Great-Granddad, even though Sean was still in the Top Twenty List of bestselling dead celebrities. Uncle Jackass made a point of forwarding me news articles every time they updated the list, as if he thought that would woo me back to music.

The suit continued, "That's why, when Professor Joshua Kim confirmed that the Hawking Wormhole leads to a parallel universe, we initiated the Classic Rock Replication program. Professor Kim?"

A balding Eurasian in high-tech clothes connected his handheld to the holoprojector. A holo of an open wormhole rotated slowly above the table. "When the Hawking Wormhole opened up a couple of years ago, astrophysicists everywhere jumped for joy. When our probes passed through the wormhole intact, we jumped a little higher. But when we confirmed the existence of a parallel universe on the other side—well, let's just say we all felt like we were floating in a null-grav field!" He smiled wanly. "If only we could figure out where it came from...."

"Never mind that," my uncle said. "Let's get to the good part."

Professor Kim tapped his handheld. The holo switched to a white-and-blue image of the Earth, followed by close-up footage of TwenCen-looking people and cities. I watched, fascinated, while Zoë and some other historians explained how they'd matched cars, clothing, and buildings to ones from our world's 1950s.

"We think—though no one is certain—that the correspondence between the two universes helps sustain the wormhole." Professor Kim said. "Historians from our world first visited this alternate Earth six years ago and confirmed the time periods match. It's currently early 1961 over there now."

Freaky to think you could jump back and forth almost a century by going through a tunnel in space.

But the people on the other Earth were even freakier because they were the same, at least the famous ones. JFK was alive and well. So were Presley, DiMaggio, and Monroe.

The professor tapped his handheld a final time, bringing up a distorted holo of a scruffy, longhaired, leather-wearing teenager. I recognized him immediately: my great-granddad himself, Sean Lyon, before he'd been discovered.

I didn't have all the numbers just yet, but they were adding up to something I didn't like. The first suit said, "As you all must realize, this parallel TwenCen world offers many opportunities for scientific and commercial research. We have the unique opportunity to watch some of our most creative minds at work—and to bring the raw genetic material of their greatness back to our own world for further study. We've already started that phase of the project; now it's time to expand it."

"And it's time for us to grow our business in a new direction," Guzman added.

That was the last clue I needed. In a hoarse voice, I asked, "You're planning to clone my great-grandfather, aren't you?"

The suit sneered at me. "Of course, Ms. Lyon. He was one of the best, most profitable singer/songwriters of the Twentieth Century, even though his career was cut short when a political dissident stabbed him after a concert. Think of this as his second chance at life, but this time with modern musical instruments and recording equipment available."

"Grandpa John wouldn't approve!"

"Grandpa John doesn't remember Sean very well. These days he has enough trouble remembering how to use a handheld." For a moment, Uncle Jackass sounded regretful. He seemed to enjoy running the estate, but I doubted he liked seeing his dad incapacitated from a stroke. Then Jackass smiled. "And this is my own pet project."

That I could understand. Jackass had inherited more credits than musical talent from Sean, but even though he'd stopped forcing us to listen to his songs, he still wanted to be someone important in the music industry. If my uncle couldn't be Sean himself, and if he couldn't turn me or his sons into Sean, then no wonder he wanted to build his own Sean from the DNA up. Too bad for him it wouldn't work.

"You know it won't be the real Sean." I stared at my uncle, willing him to abandon this stupid idea, but his expression didn't change. "You can't clone his environment. You can try for a singer and wind up with an artist—or maybe a hacker."

You'd think even my uncle would know a clone isn't ever exactly like the original. Clones are rare, but the first human clone—a boy dubbed "Guy" by the media to tie in with the first sheep clone Dolly—was born in the early 21st century. Others followed, inspiring a slew of papers in the science e-journals. I've read a few of them, and they all say that in every way, clones are less like the people they're cloned from than identical twins are like each other. Clones and originals don't share the same mitochondrial DNA or *in utero* environment, for instance, and they grow up with different families, surroundings, and expectations. A few news services tried to publicize these findings, but with the

Fundies so powerful, interest in science is at an all-time low, making scholarships impossible to find. That's part of the reason why I can't afford the Ph.D. program in genetics at Obama University.

"Frankly, Ms. Lyon," the suit said, steepling his fingers as he leaned toward me, "it doesn't really matter if Sean the Second—"

"Third," I said automatically.

He raised his graying eyebrows. "Third?"

"My great-grandparents had a stillborn son before they had Grandpa John. They named him Sean Franklin Lyon II."

Never try to match a Lyon at our family history; we have it shoved in our faces as soon as we can hold the child-sized guitars.

"Second, Third, it doesn't matter." The suit's tone told me he wouldn't tolerate further interruptions. "No offense, Mr. and Ms. Lyon, but a genuine clone would have much more drawing power than a mere descendant. If he has half the original's talent, our sales will skyrocket. If not, well, we can always put him on tour singing the old standards, either alone or with other classic rock clones."

As if forcing three generations of Lyons into music wasn't slavery enough. "I still think it's wrong," I said. "And as a mere descendant of the person in question, I object."

"And as another descendant of the person in question, the one with the authority to represent the Lyon Estate in this matter," Uncle Jackass paused to glare at me, "I grant my full approval."

I glared back.

He continued, "And Jo, now that you've voiced your official protest, I hope you'll settle down and cooperate."

"Why should I?"

He put on a false smile. "Because I want you to be the one to take the DNA from Sean."

"ME! Why?"

"It's as plain as the nose on your face." Jackass snickered. "You look so much like him you could pretend to be his cousin and get access to him, and with your science background, you should have no trouble taking the sample. Since you refused to finish the concert tour I arranged for you, you owe me."

"You practically forced me onto that tour; it was all your idea. Since when have the Lyons ever supported anything I wanted?"

Without changing expression, Jackass added, "If you want to donate your eggs for the cloning process or carry the child, I'll pay off your college debt and give you enough credits for grad school."

Like I hadn't heard that promise before. Do exactly what I want, and you'll be rewarded—someday. I snorted. "You ever try to change diapers and write a dissertation at the same time?"

"Oh, I'm not expecting you to raise little Sean." His eyes gleamed with greed. "I'll take care of that."

My cousins would never nominate him for Dad of the Year.

The whole idea sounded even worse than the disastrous Sean tribute tour Jackass had forced me to join when I was fifteen. I hid my hands in my lap so the others couldn't see me ball them. *He should be spending his credits on getting help for his stupid obsession, not feeding it.* But who here was going to stand up to a multi-billionaire besides me?

I took a deep breath and rose. "I don't want to have anything to do with this. If you'll excuse me, I'll go back to my sampling..."

Jackass nodded his head at Guzman. Licking his lips, Guzman said, "I'm sorry, Joanna, but it's in the best interests of Golden Helix to let you go."

I was too stunned to do anything but stare at him at first. Then anger loosened my dry throat. "You want to fire me? I'm the one who does most of the actual work down there! The others just talk all day. This is all because of him." I pointed at my uncle; he grinned like he'd guzzled a gallon of chocolate champagne.

The tips of Guzman's ears turned red, but he didn't speak.

"You don't have any reason not to go now, Jo," Jackass said.

"Oh, yes I do. What about my mother? Who's going to take care of her?"

He waved his hand. "That's what the sanitarium is for."

"I mean, who's going to visit her or run her outside errands?"

"She'll be fine. How long has she been in there anyway?"

He said it as if she didn't matter at all. Anger lit every single nerve I had on fire. If only I could kill him with my gaze.

"She's a human being, Jackass, she deserves some respect."

His eyes glinted like black ice. "It's her own fault she got TransAIDs, Jo. This isn't about her anyway. Are you going to get me my Sean clone or not?"

"Hell, no." I used a few Filipino swear words, all I knew of Baby's native language. "It's too bad Great-Granddad was murdered, but no matter what you do, you'll never get him back. You can't recreate him, and you can't make me into him. So leave me alone."

I grabbed my handheld and bolted. I rushed past Catherine's desk to the vator, then stopped. My bladder was threatening to burst open and flood my guts. I changed course and entered the women's bathroom instead.

Alone in a stall that smelled like violets, I slumped as I relieved myself. I'd really messed up this time. I'd lost my job, and Uncle Jackass would cut me out of the estate permanently—not that I'd counted on getting anything from him since refusing to go on that concert tour. Times like this made me wish my dad would stand up for me. But he didn't visit Mom in the long-term care center or even bother to handle her alimony payments himself; he let Jackass handle all that. Sometimes I thought everyone on my father's side of the family was a jerk.

The outer door swung open, but I didn't hear the click-click of Catherine's high heels. "Ms. Lyon?" Zoë asked hesitantly. "The receptionist said she saw you come in here."

No privacy anywhere. "Just call me Jo," I said. I finished, flushed, and came out to wash my hands.

Zoë fiddled with an earring. "I'm sorry about what happened back there, Jo."

"It's not your fault." Someone had left a bottle of hand lotion next to the sink, so I helped myself. Being a lab tech is hard on the skin.

"Maybe it is, in a way," she said.

I looked at her in confusion.

"Like many of Sean's fans, I can't help but think that if he hadn't been killed, things would have been a lot different. Would he have made more wonderful music, or would he have run for office, as he said he was considering in his final interview? Would he have stopped at being governor of Illinois, or gone for president of the U.S.? What would our country be like now if he'd replaced either of the Bushes, or Clinton? I guess that's why we all want him back so much. I just never thought how hard it must be to be one of his descendants, especially when you look so much like him."

I leaned against a stall. "You don't know the half of it. I can't get away from him. Ever since I was a little girl, he was all I heard about—at school, at home, every place I went, everyone compared me to Sean. Everyone on his side of the family expects me to play guitar, sing, and compose songs."

"I still listen to some of your songs. They're so...powerful, they make great workout music." Zoë smiled as if asking me to write more.

I felt my cheeks burn. "Simmer" had been my biggest hit, although it hadn't earned me much. Whenever I heard it now, I cringed. Everyone thought I'd been singing about sex, but it really had been about the anger that never died.

"I sequenced my genome myself in undergrad and proved I don't have enough of Sean's musical genes to match his talent, but no one believes me," I said. "My mom's the only one who ever treated me like just plain Jo, not Sean Lyon's great-granddaughter. He never did anything to me, and yet there are times I hate him."

I waited for her to crucify me for my blasphemy. Instead, she regarded me with sympathy in her green-brown eyes. I'm not used to kindness; it makes my eyes feel itchy. I looked away and swung my long ponytail over my shoulder to finger-comb the snarls from it.

"I wish I could take your place," Zoë said finally. "I'd give anything for the chance to travel to another, younger universe and experience the finest days of rock'n'roll myself. And to meet Sean…." Her voice trailed off with longing. "But I think it would be better for you to go back. You'd see he was just a man after all."

"Hey, if you're saying I need primal ancestor therapy or something, you can forget it. I'm fine. I can take care of myself. Been doing so ever since Mom got locked up—"

I stopped as I looked in the mirror and saw myself. Not just my features, but my expression. I wasn't fooling anyone that I was happy, not when my face looked shut-off and defensive compared to Zoë's open, serene face. I tried smiling and was appalled by how unnatural it felt. Was I really going around looking so sullen? No wonder I hadn't had a date in over a year.

Maybe Zoë had a point. Maybe I should go back and yell at Great-Granddad Sean for messing up our whole family. Wouldn't change my own past, of course, since he would be in a parallel universe, but it might make me feel better. Or who knows, maybe I'd prove I'd inherited his genes for anger. I managed a genuine smile at that thought. But it faded as I remembered what the trip was really about. Uncle Jackass was the last person who ought to have any contact with Sean—or Sean's clone. The poor kid was going to grow up more twisted than a double helix. I didn't want anything to do with this project, but Jackass would still do it even without me. Maybe if I pretended to go along with him for now, I could find some way to sabotage the project later. Now that was something to smile about.

"All right, I'll do it," I said. "The DNA retrieval, that is, not the egg donor or surrogate mother part. But I can't go back and face Uncle Jackass and all those suits. Could you tell them for me?"

She smiled in return. "You made the right decision, Jo, you'll see. I'll be happy to tell them."

Her hand was on the door when inspiration struck. "But maybe you should make it sound like I'm not sure," I said. "Tell my uncle that I'll only do it if he finally makes that donation to the TransAIDS Foundation."

She laughed and hummed a few bars of Sean's "Money's Not My Master" before she left.

When I was alone, I stared at my reflection again. "All right, Great-Granddad," I whispered. "You and me, one on one. We'll see if nature really is stronger than nurture. And we'll see if I can stop Uncle Jackass's crazy plan."

CHAPTER TWO

Guzman wasn't kidding when he said the ship was leaving in a few days; as soon as I agreed to go, the suits sent me running around for paperwork and physicals and all that nonsense. What with sorting, packing, and sending most of my things to storage, not to mention getting out of my lease and handling all of the other last-minute details, I was lucky if I got three hours of sleep a night. Maybe it was a good thing I'd lost my job; I don't think I could have managed everything if I'd been working.

The afternoon before I departed for the *Sagan*, I hired a self-driving car and programmed it with my mother's address. As the car zipped north, past abandoned suburbs converted to mini-farms, I scarfed down a sandwich, then dozed until the car woke me up by saying, "You've reached your destination."

The sanitarium was housed in what used to be a resort hotel, in the middle of a wildlife refuge. I stared at the spindly trees as the car navigated the long, twisting driveway. It was hard to believe a grand forest had once stood here, even though I'd seen photos of the resort during its TwenCen heyday. The area still supported more plants and animals than the parks in Chicago. I always thought it was a shame my mom and the other patients weren't allowed outside to enjoy nature. They had to rely on caretakers to bring flowers into the lobby.

I checked into the security system with my ID and a retina scan, and the holo of a broadly smiling Asian woman directed me to a visiting room. I already knew my way to the women visitors' locker area, where I showered and changed into disposable shirt and pants, tightening them with tabs, before heading to my designated meeting area. Normally when I visited Mom, I came in the afternoon so we could share an English tea on opposite sides of the glass wall. This time, it was already after dinner. I ordered tea for two anyway, but the drinks arrived before my mother. She used a walker like a much older woman, and she winced with each step.

"Mom?" I rose before I remembered I couldn't reach her through the barrier. "What happened? Are you OK?"

She rolled her eyes. "I'm perfectly fine, Jo—as fine as I can ever be in this prison. I just need a little more help getting around these days, that's all."

Mom was as poor a liar as I am. Her clothes blanketed her, and her eyebrows and hair were sparser than I remembered, even if they were still the same sandy brown. I'd wondered before if she tried to hide how serious her condition was with clothes and makeup during my scheduled visits; her appearance seemed to confirm my hypothesis.

She eased herself into an overstuffed chair next to the barrier. "What are you doing up here on a weekday? Did something happen?"

I couldn't help laughing. "You could say that." I summarized my meeting with Guzman and my uncle. She frowned when I described what Jackass wanted me to do.

"I hope you told him where he could stick his clone," she said.

"Yeah, but...." I looked down at my mug. "I told him I'd go."

"Joanna Maribel Lyon, what in the world got into you? I can't believe you're supporting the Lyon family, especially Jack."

I wanted to tell her about my plan to backstab Jackass, but I didn't dare. Mom wouldn't tell him, but he might have a spy at the sanitarium. "I'm not supporting them. I'm just going to get him to give me some of the credits I deserve." Despite Mom's scowl, I stared at her. "And I made him promise to donate some credits to the TransAIDS Foundation."

Her scowl softened, though it didn't disappear. "You didn't have to do that."

"I wanted to."

She waved my help away with a bony hand. "Jo, the only way I'm going to leave this place is if they ever figure out how to stop this damn virus from spreading. If I'm really lucky, they'll find a cure, but then I'll still have to go through rehab to get rid of this walker."

"Stop talking like you're old, Mom. You have decades ahead of you yet."

"At the rate they're going, I'll be lucky if they can cure me before I'm ninety." She pointed at me. "You're the one who still has a future. You should be focusing on that. If you love science so much, you should go get your Ph.D., not run stupid errands for your crazy uncle."

"Well, when I come back, I'll have enough credits for grad school, so it all works out."

Mom sat silently for a moment. Then she said, "You be careful out there. Spaceships, wormholes, the TwenCen…it can all be very dangerous."

This from the woman who always came up with a different explanation as to how she'd become infected with the TransAIDS virus.

We chatted for a few more minutes about her freelance holo design work, but I was too tired to pay much attention. After I yawned for the third time, Mom set aside her mug. "You should get going, Jo. You've got a very long trip ahead of you." She kissed her fingers and laid her hand against the barrier; I copied her. Her hands were a fraction longer than mine, and her long nails glittered like gems. "I love you, dear. Stay safe."

"You too, Mom."

We stared at each other as if daring the other to leave first. I felt like I should say something else, but my throat felt too narrow to let a single syllable escape. If I swallowed, I'd choke.

"Don't cry, Joanna," Mom whispered.

Yeah, don't cry. That was what my parents had told me right after they announced their divorce, whenever I got bullied at school, when Uncle Jackass yelled at me for not practicing guitar every minute I was awake. Crying was weak; crying wouldn't get you anything. Crying wouldn't have helped my mom when she was first diagnosed. And it wouldn't have stopped her from turning around and making her slow exit, never looking back.

I watched every step of hers until the door closed behind her. Then I shoved at the glass barrier as hard as I could. It didn't even quiver; it had been reinforced to be virtually unbreakable.

I leaned against the glass and wished I was that shatterproof. I stayed there for a couple of minutes. Anger at the whole world spun itself into a protective scowl. If I'd met anyone in the locker room or the parking lot, I would have spat at them for saying hello. Instead, I kicked the tires of my hired car over and over, until my foot was sore and I was tired enough to crawl inside and let it take me home.

* * *

I woke up in front of my apartment building. I checked my handheld to make sure I'd paid for the car and saw "Urgent Message from Ian Lyon" flashing red on the screen. Had I damaged my handheld, or I was still asleep and having a bad dream? When was the last time Dad had contacted me? Had he found out about my mission for Uncle Jackass? I wasn't up to dealing with Dad, no matter how urgent his message was. I deleted it and returned to packing.

Ten hours later, after a short night's sleep and a much longer train ride, I arrived at Columbia Spaceport, where I'd board a space plane that would take me directly to the *Sagan*. My uncle had sent one of his assistants to help expedite me through the final security checks and luggage inspection. He even gave me access to the first-class lounge, where they served me lobster rolls, champagne, and chocolate truffles. I half-expected one of them to open up and reveal a not-so-subtle fortune: *You can get a lot more luxury in your life if you do what your nice, rich uncle wants.* Yeah, as if pricey food was worth more than freedom. I'd rather wade through nutrient broth naked than go on a concert tour, stuck in hotel rooms for my own security and forced to play the same songs that I didn't care about over and over. Only by leaving the lounge and getting a cup of herbal tea was I able to keep my lunch down.

The space plane didn't have windows; instead, I and the rest of the passengers got to see a real-time holo of the *Sagan*. The holo grew larger and more detailed as we came closer. The ship itself reminded me of a slightly deflated ball with wings. I wondered what color the outer shell was in real life; in the holo, it was steel-blue. I couldn't gauge the size of the ship from the holo, though the briefing materials had said it was as big as a city-ship. However, instead of featuring lots of entertainment centers and restaurants, the Sagan included several fish ponds, gardens, and labs. One of my cousins hadn't left the city-ship where he performed since he moved there six years ago. He had the opportunity to leave at any port; I'd be stuck inside this spaceship for six months. I wondered how the crew who lived here managed to stay sane.

The plane docked in a hangar, gliding in so smoothly it took me a few seconds to realize that we'd stopped. I lined up with the other passengers, but I waited a half hour before I finally got to the front of the line. One crew member scanned my ID while a nurse took a blood sample and measured my vitals.

"You're all set, Ms. Lyon." The crew member returned my handheld. "Do you have your room assignment and orientation documents?"

I did, but I'd only looked at my room assignment. I nodded anyway.

"Good. Dr. Pluckenreck will be available to answer any questions you have." She smiled. "Welcome aboard your home away from home."

And that was that, not a reference to Sean Lyon anywhere. My carisaks felt a little lighter than they had a few moments ago.

My quarters were four levels up from the hangar. The door slid open and then invited me to set the lock with a retinal scan. I had a firmfoam bed that folded into the wall, several storage cubes, and a workstation with a table and chair that locked into the floor. The main area was about twice as long as I was, and I could touch opposite walls in the bathroom by stretching out my arms. No wonder they'd advised me to travel light. I didn't think I'd want to spend much time in here.

I lay down for an hour, but it was impossible to rest in a strange, blank room, especially with odd rattling noises startling me every time my eyes shut. After the fifth or sixth time that happened, I decided to stop worrying the ship was going to fall apart and leave me floating in space. I unpacked and set up some of my favorite holos: a picture of Mom and ten-year-old me at an amusement park, an artificially colored double helix, and reproductions of my favorite paintings: "The Scream" and "The Starry Night." That was better, but I still felt like getting out of my cube. I linked into the *Sagan's* server and downloaded a map. There were plenty of places to check out, such as the mess hall, the garden, and a rec area, but what caught my eye was the genetics lab. I hoped they wouldn't mind if I paid them a visit.

Every level on the *Sagan* was a different color. The corridors on the science/medical level were painted pale blue with white doors. The door to the genetics lab was partway open, allowing me to hear voices over an old opera playing in the background. I peeked in.

The lab seemed to be nothing but boxes at first, covering the lab benches and blocking the narrow aisles. A portly, balding man, pencil-like scanner in one hand and handheld in the other, squeezed through the gaps, scanning each box and identifying its contents for the tall, black-haired woman following him.

"Petri dishes. Verify?"

"Verified," the woman replied after opening the box in question.

"How many? Did we receive all that we paid for?"

"You know I'm not going to count them, Ferdie!"

"But how else will we know if we have enough for the trip? Supply companies don't deliver out by the wormhole!"

"It's too late for other deliveries anyway." The woman picked up an open box and started to move it closer to the door. She saw me before I could flee. "Hello," she said. "Don't I know you from somewhere?"

I shook my head; I didn't want to get into explanations.

"Is that the new lab tech?" Ferdie asked, not turning around.

The woman turned back to him. "Don't you remember? She got bumped at the last minute for that traveler."

Ferdie swore in German.

I wondered uneasily if they were talking about me. "Actually, I used to be a lab tech back at Golden Helix."

The woman glanced at Ferdie, then approached me. "A lab tech? What's your name?"

"Joanna Lyon, but everyone calls me Jo."

The woman raised her eyebrows, but if she recognized my surname, she didn't comment on it. "I'm Elizabeth Tappen. So, what did you do at GH, Jo?"

"Mostly I sampled developing organs, with some occasional work in testing experimental media and additives."

"Any cell work? DNA analysis? Cloning?"

I winced at the mention of cloning. "I did some DNA analysis in undergrad, but I'm out of practice."

"Some is better than none. Who was your boss?"

Why did she want to know? Could she be offering me a job? I tried not to assume anything, but excitement tickled my throat. "Rhonda Banerjee."

"Thanks. If you'll excuse me..."

Elizabeth retreated to the back of the lab. I wondered if she was calling my supervisor. At least Rhonda had appreciated me, even if Guzman and my co-workers hadn't. Ferdie had gone back to scanning boxes. I wasn't sure if I should interrupt him, so I put my hands in my pocket and pushed my way through the maze, examining the lab equipment on the benches. Cell and DNA prep stations, sequencers and analyzers, microcentrifuges...they all reminded me of the science labs I'd studied in, even though these machines were newer. I itched to use them.

Elizabeth returned, grinning. "Rhonda spoke highly of you, Jo. She said she complained to upper management when they let you go, but they wouldn't listen to her. How about it, Ferdie?"

"How about what?"

"How about we take Jo on as a part-time tech, at least for now?" She turned back to me. "That is, if you're interested—and if Dr. Pluckenreck lets you. You are one of the travelers, correct?"

"If you mean one of the people who's supposed to go to the other Earth, then yeah."

She peered at me. "What's your mission?"

"I'm…meeting my ancestor."

"That's it? They normally don't encourage that sort of thing. Who is it?"

I repressed a sigh. "Sean Lyon, the musician."

Elizabeth and Ferdie both went still for a moment. Then she said, "I thought you looked familiar. Maybe that's why."

Ferdie rubbed his hands together with an expectant air. "Are you going to record some of his music? I love the classics!"

"He played rock'n'roll, not opera," Elizabeth said. "Are you a musician too? I didn't think the travelers were arranging music lessons now, but it wouldn't surprise me."

I didn't want to share with them the repugnant mission my uncle had assigned me, or my secret one. What could I say? After a few seconds of tapping my fingers while I thought, I forced my hands to stay still. Maybe I could tell them the truth, just not the whole truth. "I used to play guitar, but I gave it up. I prefer genetics."

Elizabeth perked up. "Where'd you get your Ph.D. from?"

"I don't have it yet."

Ferdie and Elizabeth looked at each other, then Ferdie put his scanner down and stuck out his red, meaty hand. "There aren't nearly enough scientists to go around these days, and anything we can do to get another one off of the ground…ah, we are off of the ground, aren't we?" He chuckled. "Perhaps we can steal you away from Pluckenreck. Would you be interested in helping us out? Maybe we can set up some classes for you through Net University in return."

"I…I'd love to." What had I done for them to be so nice to me?

"Welcome to our lab, Jo. I'm Ferdinand Hessthal, but everyone calls me Ferdie. I manage this lab—and Lizabeth manages me."

I beamed for about a minute before he thrust a pair of safety glasses at me. "You can start by helping us put all our supplies away, before the others come in and waste them."

It was a good way to learn the layout of the lab, though at times it was almost impossible to open the cabinets. Before long, we uncovered a stack of perishable items mixed in with the normal equipment. I had to take the perishables to the walk-in cooler, which felt more like Antarctica than a mere cooler. A lab coat had been abandoned on a bench, so I borrowed it, rolling up the sleeves before returning to work.

I was squatting in the cooler, organizing reagents on the bottom shelf, when I heard the door open behind me. "Er, excuse me," a man said in an appealingly low voice, "I think you've got my lab coat."

CHAPTER THREE

I turned around and looked up at one of the cutest scientists I've ever seen. He had reddish highlights in his otherwise light brown hair, which was cut short but still wavy. His face was strong and gentle, and his mouth looked like it laughed a lot. His eyes—deep blue, sheltered by long, dark, eyelashes—widened as he looked at me.

"Oh, I'm sorry," he said. "Lizabeth just said Jo took it, so I thought you were a boy Joe, not a girl Jo."

"Uh, yeah, I'm a girl." Where was the famed Lyon wit when I needed it? "Last time I checked, anyway."

He smiled. I liked the way he smiled; he did it with his whole face.

I left the chemicals on the floor and stood up. "Sorry about taking your coat, but I didn't want to become part of any cryogenics experiments you were running in here. I'm almost done; you can have it back." I hesitated before undoing the top button. Despite the chill, my face felt flushed. I was wearing jeans and a short-sleeved turtleneck under the lab coat; why did I feel like I was doing a striptease?

"No, no, that's all right. It looks better on you than me. I mean, I don't need it this afternoon. I'm just sequencing a couple of mutants I've been working on."

He was babbling too, I realized. He must not meet that many women in space. I looked down at the lab coat, trying to read the blue, upside-down embroidery. "You must be…George, then?"

"Yeah." His grin widened, as if he were trying not to blurt out the punchline of a joke. "I'm George Harrison."

"No, you're not," I said before I realized it. Damn it, this wasn't the kind of Lyon wit I wanted to display!

He didn't seem to mind. "I'm not the guitar player, or even a relative. My mom named me for him, since we share the same birthday."

"Boy, I'd have killed my mom if she had done that to me." Mom always said my dad had picked out my name while she was still doped up from giving birth, claiming it was family tradition to pass on some form of Sean's name. Since "Sean" was the Irish form of "John," my relatives had names like Jack, Ian, Johan, Evan, and so on. Sometimes I wished Mom had refused to call me Joanna, but I'd never been able to decide on a name that fit me better.

"Actually, it inspired me to play guitar when I was in school. I wasn't great, but it was fun." He raised his dark eyebrows. "But Ferdie said there are two musicians in the lab now."

No getting away from it, not even with a cute guy. I took a deep breath. "My name is Joanna Lyon."

"Really? Are you related to Sean Lyon?"

"I'm his great-granddaughter. Can't you tell?"

He reached for me. I wasn't sure what he meant to do; part of me wanted to flee or hurl insults at him. I had to force myself to remain still and trust him.

He nudged my cap off of my face. "Well, yes, you do look like him," he said, "only you're much prettier."

My face burned hot enough to set the cooler on fire. No one ever looked at me for prettiness, just traces of Great-Granddad.

I was trying to think of a graceful response to his compliment when my stomach grumbled. "Did you miss lunch?" George asked.

With all the traveling, I had no idea what mealtime it was anymore. "I haven't eaten since the spaceport."

"What was Ferdie thinking, putting you to work without letting you eat first! If you can wait ten more minutes while I load the sequencer, I can show you around the mess hall."

"That'd be great." I hurried to put the rest of the chemicals away. "I'll see you out there."

My two new supervisors were a little too eager to send us off to lunch together.

* * *

I spent most of the next few days in the lab practicing cutting and splicing DNA and transferring it into cells. I hadn't had much chance to perform these techniques since undergrad, and though everyone, especially George, was eager to help me, I wanted to prove myself by doing them on my own.

They'd given me a lab bench in the back of the lab, close to the cooler. I was peering through my microscope, trying to inject DNA into a mouse cell, when my handheld blared, "Urgent message for Ms. Lyon! Acknowledgement required!"

I was so startled I shot the DNA into the media, not the cell. I bit back a curse and checked my handheld. A holo appeared of a graying woman in a TwenCen suit—with a skirt. A pair of gold-colored spectacles hung from a chain around her neck. Maybe she was pretending to be a businesswoman on the TwenCen Earth, but to me, she looked more like a prison warden searching for escapees.

"Ms. Lyon, my records indicate you did not attend the orientation session for universe travelers this morning. Instead, you were in the genetics lab." Her scowl deepened. "I don't know what you're doing there, but that's not part of your job. You won't be allowed to visit the alternate Earth if you miss your sessions."

Some threat. I would have been happier to erase the whole Sean Lyon mission like a strand of error-ridden DNA. But when I paused the message and looked away, everyone else in the lab was staring at me.

Ferdie spoke as if he were giving a eulogy at a wake. "You'll have to do what Dr. Pluckenreck says, Jo. Technically, you're a traveler, not crew."

"That doesn't mean we have to lose her, does it?" George asked.

"Depends on her schedule," Lizabeth said.

I pulled up the schedule I'd been ignoring. Speech training, history, the money system, wardrobe...I'd be spending more time training to meet Sean than actually being with him.

"Ridiculous." I brandished my handheld and wished Pluckenreck were here in person so I could hurl it at her. "It's like they think I know nothing at all about TwenCen Earth."

George came over and grabbed my arm. "Careful of the glassware. Did you double-major in genetics and history? Maybe you could test out of some of the classes."

Now that was a good idea. I hadn't formally studied history, but I'd seen and read so many bios of Sean I knew some of the material. "I'll ask Pluckenreck after the afternoon class."

* * *

After lunch with George, I remained in the mess hall, since the travelers' class would be held there. About thirty other people gathered in a corner, so I shifted my seat to be near them, in the back. It still wasn't enough to hide me from Pluckenreck. As soon as she arrived, she scanned the crowd with her handheld. A notice popped up on my handheld, indicating I'd been credited with attendance for Time Travel Ethics 101. "So nice to see we have full attendance today," Pluckenreck said. She stared at me for a moment, but I didn't look away. I'd met her power-hungry type before. If she was going to be petty, then that gave me more reason to test out of her classes—if she let me.

Pluckenreck stood in front of an ocean mural as she lectured us on what to do once we arrived on the alternate Earth. It wasn't enough to learn how people acted during that time; we had to limit ourselves to their tech and knowledge too. We couldn't tell anyone about our computers or medicine—and we especially couldn't tell people what would happen to them or about upcoming historical events, even if that meant people would die.

"I know it sounds cruel." She put on a frown that probably was supposed to make her seem concerned and sympathetic. Instead, it looked fake. "There are so many people who died in natural disasters or by violence that could be saved if we warned them. But can they really be saved?" She shrugged. "So far, everything we've seen indicates that the history of this Earth matches our own in every detail we can compare. Our physicists think the similarity allowed the wormhole to open in the first place. If something significant is changed—like saving a person's life—it could ripple out in ways we can't predict. Maybe the wormhole will be stable; maybe it will collapse, and we'll have to spend the rest of our lives there. No one wants to take that chance. Any questions?"

A guy about my age who was sitting up front stuck out his hand. "How do we know we're not altering the past just by being here?"

"You're not the first group we've allowed to visit the TwenCen Earth. When we started, our missions were much smaller and heavily supervised. We bought as many newspapers and magazines as possible, watched news broadcasts, and listened to whatever we could. But nothing changed; everything still matches our past. We're counting on all of you to keep it that way." She found me again. "No matter who you know who's going to die young."

What an asshole. She was telling me straight out I couldn't save Sean. It hadn't occurred to me before, but now I wanted to, if only to piss Pluckenreck off. But I knew better than to say anything, so I just glared at her.

After she resumed her lecture, I remembered my plan to ask her about testing out of some of the classes. Shit; I'd gotten her annoyed at me before I'd even spoken to her. Was it even worth talking to her now? I thought about spending time with George and performing experiments in the genetics lab. I couldn't give them up without at least trying to persuade Pluckenreck.

I watched her like a model student, but the only other thing she said that sank in was that there'd be a few exceptions to the TwenCen-tech-only rule. She finished by saying she'd bring along some disguised technology for us to play with next time. Most of the other students left. A few hung around to talk to Pluckenreck, but I pressed against the wall to watch. To them, she was polite, taking the time to answer their questions. But when the last one left and I came forward, she turned away and fussed with her handheld.

"Dr. Pluckenreck? I'm Joanna Lyon. I wanted to talk to you about my schedule...."

"You can access the classes you missed on the *Sagan's* server," she said, still not facing me.

"I will. But I've looked at the rest of the syllabus, and since I already know a lot about history, I was wondering if I could skip some of the classes...."

Now she turned to scowl at me. "Absolutely not."

"But I already know a lot about Sean's era...."

"Maybe, but it won't be enough. Do you know how to use a rotary phone, dollar bills and coins, and paper books? Do you know what entertainers are most popular, and for what? If I gave you a dress, would you know how to put it on?"

I hadn't thought about the day-to-day details. I'd read about the era, seen holos, and even handled some of Sean's belongings, but I didn't know how to use them. I shook my head after each question.

"That's why you need training." Now her scowl had turned into a smirk. "And you'll have to demonstrate you can do all that before we arrive at the other Earth."

"What happens if I can't?"

"Then we can't let you complete your mission, and the ISA will expect you to pay for your trip into space."

I didn't want to know how much that would cost. I knew I could never earn that many credits on my own.

"Mr. Jack Lyon will be very disappointed, too." Her voice was casual, but her eyes pierced me like lasers.

"I see," I told her. What I really saw was that my uncle had recruited a watchdog to make sure I did what he wanted.

Pluckenreck left. I ordered a cup of black coffee and sat with it in front of me for a long time, staring at the starscape projected one of the walls. Part of me wished I'd never entered the genetics lab so I wouldn't know what—and who—I had to give up. The other part of me tried to plot a way to make things work—and get away from Pluckenreck. In the end, all I could come up with was the resolution to help out in the lab during my off hours, if they would still take me.

* * *

Ferdie and Lizabeth looked disappointed when I told them about Pluckenreck's refusal to let me test out of some of the classes, but they agreed to let me work part-time as long as someone else was in the lab. "For safety," Lizabeth said. Since the scientists tended to work long hours anyway, it wasn't an issue. So for the next couple of months I juggled classes during the day and lab work at night. Even though I spent most of my time with the other travelers, I felt more at home with Ferdie, Lizabeth, Lizabeth's wife Olivia, and George. Especially George. But George and I did disagree on one major thing: music. He liked to play guitar and sing, and I didn't. When I told George I hadn't brought a guitar with me, he said he understood why, but he frowned first. And every time he sang one of his namesake's songs, I remembered the disastrous concert tour Great-Uncle Jack had insisted I go on as a teenager, when he'd tried to make me into someone I wasn't.

"Can't you sing something else?" I complained to George one morning. I'd broken three big beakers in half an hour, and Ferdie had yelled at me. He'd apologized afterward, but my nerves still felt sharp. George's choice of "Slivers in My Soul" cut too close to the bone.

He broke off his tune, his blue eyes wide with puzzlement. "But Sean had nothing to do with that song."

"It's still from his era." I inspected my fourth beaker for hairline cracks. I didn't want this one to split while I was heating my solution. "I don't want Great-Granddad in my face all the time."

"What's so bad about it? I get the comparisons to the original George Harrison all the time." He drew closer. "You can change your face and your name, Jo, but you can't change your ancestry. Why not just accept it and go on with your life?"

I glared at him. "Because no one expects you to replace Guitar George like the way they expect me to replace my great-granddad."

George didn't sing at all for the rest of the day; when he had to speak to me, he did so in flat monosyllables. I felt like I'd broken more than just a few pieces of glass—like I'd broken the harmony of the lab, or worse yet, the still fragile harmony between George and myself.

* * *

The next day I had a session with Wardrobe so they could alter my costumes. The getup they made me wear was ridiculous, all dresses and skirts with sweaters, no jeans or slacks of any kind. At least my outfits weren't as exotic as Winnie's. She was staying for a full year in Africa, collecting DNA samples from endangered species. The Wardrobe specialists, a middle-aged woman who favored long scarves and a tall, thin man who reminded me of a crane, argued for ten minutes about which costumes they should give her before the man stomped off to the storage room.

"How are you going to handle the different languages?" I asked Winnie while the Wardrobe woman rummaged through her storage cabinets for shoes that would fit me.

"I learned them before I even applied for this mission." She bounced up and down on the soles of her feet.

"You must have really wanted the job," I said.

"Oh, yeah. I've seen documentaries of the great animal herds before, but it'll be amazing to see them in person. And to think I'll be able to help save them by collecting their DNA."

I couldn't help smiling at her enthusiasm. "Maybe I'll get to sequence the DNA when you bring it in."

"You're still working in the lab? Do you actually like it there, or is it just to get closer to that guy you're seeing?"

Wardrobe Woman returned, carrying an armload of transparent shoe boxes. Most of the shoes were black and brown, but they all had high heels.

"Don't you have any flats?" I asked Wardrobe Woman.

She shook her head. "Women of this era generally wear heels with this type of dress."

Winnie craned her neck to inspect my shoes. "That's nothing, Jo."

"It's still higher than what I'm used to."

"Then you'll need to practice walking in them." Wardrobe Woman selected a pair and gave the shoes to me. I stepped into them warily. Standing up wasn't too bad, but I only got halfway to the door before a heel slipped out from under me. My leg followed the shoe, and I had to grab onto Winnie to stop myself from falling.

"You really do need practice," she said once we'd sorted ourselves out and I'd apologized.

"Well, I'm not wearing them to the lab."

She winked. "Then how about for George?"

I didn't want to tell her about our argument the day before. I didn't think she'd understand. So I paced up and down the room while the Wardrobe people fussed over Winnie. I couldn't stop thinking about the argument. How was George able to be so nonchalant about being named after a famous guitarist? He hadn't grown up being expected to replace said guitarist, so he had no idea what it was like. Still, I envied his serenity. I missed him too.

I changed into my normal clothes for my next lecture, but I couldn't stop thinking about George. Finally, I decided I owed it to him to apologize. But I didn't want to do it in the lab; I wanted to make it something special.

I returned to Wardrobe and checked out a red, clingy dress that had already been set aside for me. I had a white sweater to wear over it, for modesty, but I decided I didn't want to wear it. Back in my cabin, I carefully pulled on fragile stockings, a garter belt and the lethal heels, then donned some of my own silver jewelry. I tried putting my hair up, but it was too long to manage. I finally just twisted it over my shoulder.

"Not bad, Joanna, not bad at all," I said after viewing myself in my tiny mirror. "I don't think too many people will compare you to Great-Granddad tonight."

That's when I heard the opening chords of Sean's "Let's Rebegin" outside my door. A few bars later, George sang:

I didn't think you would take it so hard

I didn't know that I'd played my last card

If you're an angel, please forgive my sin,

Let's take it from the top, let's rebegin...

My cheeks grew warm. It wasn't one of my favorite Sean songs, and George omitted a few notes, but that didn't matter. George was singing an apology to me. I pressed myself against the door so I could listen.

After the chorus, George stopped playing and cleared his throat. "I'm sorry, Jo. I guess it was a stupid idea to sing you one of Sean's songs when you hate him so much. It seemed like the right thing to say..."

His voice trailed off. Had he left? Sudden fear made me scramble to open the door, but my fingers trembled on the panel. By the time the door slid open, George was walking toward the vator. "George, wait!" I called.

He turned, then stopped, gaze fixed on me. I couldn't help returning the favor. He had spiffed himself up too, with a haircut and neatly pressed white shirt and gray pants. Traces of his musky aftershave still lingered by the entrance. Clipped to his DNA-patterned tie was a white flower from the hydroponic gardens.

"You're beautiful," he blurted out. Milliseconds later, his face was bright pink. I think mine must have matched it.

He tried again. "I'm sorry, Jo. I wanted to apologize for making you think I was comparing you to your great-granddad, but I guess I can't even do that without bringing him into the picture."

"It's all right," I said. "I was going to apologize to you too, for snapping at you."

We stared at each other for a few more minutes before he said, "You really do look wonderful. Did you dress up for me?"

"Yeah. And...did you dress up for me?"

"Yeah." He paused. "May I take you out to dinner then, at our lavish, five-star mess hall?"

"I'd be delighted," I said.

"The pleasure is mine. Do you mind if I leave my guitar in your room?"

As long as he didn't expect me to play it. "No, that's fine."

"I wasn't sure what'd you think," he said as he set his guitar inside the door. "Oh, and this is for you." He unclipped his flower from his tie and attempted to fasten it to my dress with his tie clip. I tucked it behind my ear.

Since it was past the supper rush, the mess hall was mostly deserted. There wasn't much of a selection: a few hard rolls, cooling vegetable soup, wilting salad, meatloaf, and a few pieces of cherry pie. I helped myself to everything but the pie and followed George to a corner table with a starscape hanging above it.

"Watch the floor," he said, "it's wet…"

With impeccable timing, the stupid shoes slipped. I almost did the splits as I fell onto my tray. China crunched under me.

"Damn it!" I yelled. "I wasn't this clumsy before I came onboard!"

George hurried towards me. "Jo? Are you all right?"

I rolled off the tray and surveyed the damage. My leg muscles felt strained, but not badly. What food I wasn't wearing was completely inedible, and George's flower was floating in the soup. The front of my dress was sopping wet, a carrot had wormed its way into my bra, and ranch-flavored lettuce was clinging to my face.

George started picking up the scattered pieces of china. "Are you all right, Jo?" he asked again.

"I won't be," I said, brushing noodles out of my hair.

"You won't be?"

"Yeah. When Wardrobe hears about this, they'll expect me to fix my clothes. And I sew like I walk in heels."

He tilted his head back and laughed. I glared at him, then threw a soup noodle at his face. It clung to his cheek, but he was laughing too hard to brush it off. Finally, I started laughing myself. I took my shoes off and brandished them, spiky heels first. "Let Pluckenreck come after me! I'll poke her eyes out!" George's face turned bright pink, which made me laugh harder. We sat there for a couple of minutes like that; every time one of us started to calm down, we'd look at the other one and crack up again.

I don't think I'd laughed like that for a long time.

When we could breathe normally again, we cleaned up as much of the mess as we could. Then we went back to my cubicle, my shoes in one hand and my other one on George's arm. We never did eat dinner that night. Instead, we made love for the first time.

George wasn't the first guy I'd slept with, nor—to be honest—was he the most skilled. But he was loving, and he was unexpectedly sensual, and he made the physical act of sex into something more, a private celebration made more joyful by its spontaneity. As we lay there afterwards, trying a new contortion every minute as we struggled to fit two people into a half-person cot, I decided I wouldn't mind having him around for the next forty years or so.

As long as we got a bigger bed.

* * *

A few days later, I was catching up on my messages from Earth over breakfast. In my normal clothes, the mess hall floor presented no hazard, and soon I was hunched over my handheld, skimming messages between bites of a bagel and yogurt blended with fruit. Winnie and a couple of other travelers waved at me as they came in. I waved back and returned to my messages.

There was a short note from Mom asking how my trip was going, without mentioning anything about her life.

I checked out of messages and skimmed the month-old news stories. At first, they all seemed the same as always: more political battles between the Fundie and PC parties, more physical battles in the MidEast, more environmental devastation in Africa and Asia. Then a flagged story picked up by my personal search engine caught my eye: "*E. coli* Outbreak in TransAIDS Long-Term Care Clinic; Deliberate Introduction by Extremist."

Oh my God. Mom….

My hands shook so badly I had trouble scrolling the story. Police had picked up an extremist Fundie woman claiming to be the Wrath of God, sent to Earth to purge it. She'd managed to penetrate the quarantine surrounding the clinic where my mom was. Before she'd been caught, the dammed Fundie had infected the water supply with a virulent strain of bacteria. By the time the article had been uploaded, over ninety percent of the patients and staff had been infected. There was no word in this story on deaths, but I knew they were inevitable. One of Mom's friends at the clinic had died of simple food poisoning; something like this would probably wipe out the entire clinic.

The yogurt suddenly tasted bitter, almost noxious, and the coffee only made it worse. I clutched the warm cup tightly and stared into the coffee, wishing it could show me Mom's face. I set my handheld to chime the millisecond messages or updates on the story came through, then went to class.

CHAPTER FOUR

The message came that evening, while I was studying a gene sequence that looked more like alphabet soup than a protein recipe. I'd kept my handheld next to me on the benchtop so I could grab it in a microsecond. Even so, the chimes blended in with the plaintive duet coming from Ferdie's own handheld. I grabbed my handheld and opened the message, hoping it meant Mom was OK. Instead, I read:

Dear Ms. Lyon,

It is with deepest sympathy that we inform you of the death of your mother, Cassandra Wells-Lyon…

I couldn't help it; I screamed. Halfway through, I changed it to a more acceptable "Fuck." Then I couldn't stop myself: "Fuck, fuck, fuck, fuck, fuck…"

"Jo, stop that." Lizabeth looked up from her microscope, eyes narrowed in irritation. "Whatever went wrong, you can always do the experiment over again."

"No, I can't." I laughed; even to me, it sounded brittle, forced. "If only it was just an experiment gone wrong."

George stopped at my bench, a rack of test tubes in his hand. "What happened, Jo?"

"My mom…my mom…."

I couldn't finish the sentence; it would have made the whole thing real, not just another piece of downloaded news. My throat felt like it was swollen shut. I pushed my handheld over to George. Lizabeth craned her neck, and they read the message together.

Lizabeth reacted first. "Oh, Jo, that's so awful. And telling you by message—maybe I'm TwenCen about this, but I think bad news ought to be delivered in person, or at least over the cel. Guess that's hard when we're so far from Earth."

Lizabeth's rambling was preferable to what George did. Murmuring "I'm here for you, Jo," he pulled me into his embrace, smothering me in bleach-scented lab coat and the warmth of his body. Smothering me in comfort, tempting me to be vulnerable.

Don't cry, Joanna.

I was stiff in his arms; I didn't even know how to let myself relax. I wouldn't have dared to even if I could; I didn't want George to think me weak.

"Jo? Joanna? It's alright." George stroked my hair from the crown of my head to the small of my back. "Lizabeth's not going to mind if we hold each other here in the lab, right, Lizabeth?"

"Of course not. Just don't make a habit of it."

Even her light tone couldn't make me react.

"I think you'd better take Jo to her cubicle, George." Lizabeth whispered, but I still heard her. "She's in shock. Call the med lab if she gets worse. I'll tell Ferdie not to expect her to work for a few days."

George led me out of there, still in our lab coats and safety glasses. When we got to my cubicle, he helped me take them off, then my shoes and the rest of my clothes, finally tucking me in. All the while he talked softly to me or held my hand. But though I let him strip my body, he couldn't uncover my heart.

* * *

"God damn it, Jo." I flinched just as much from his words as from his sharp tone; George almost never swore. "Stop acting like you're made of computer chips. I know there's a human inside of you somewhere; why won't you let me see her?"

It had been two days since I'd heard the news. I'd spent them in my quarters, mostly staring at holos of Mom or reading her old messages. George had been there whenever he could, and Winnie and some of the other travelers had stopped by as well. Even Pluckenreck had sent condolences. I was getting sick of putting on a brave face for all of them, getting sick of staring at my holo of Munch's "The Scream." Helping George secure the lab equipment before the *Sagan* passed through the wormhole had seemed like a good idea—until he started ragging on me.

"You should know by now I'm human," I said. "You've seen me break enough glassware." I zipped my microscope into its padded case and placed it in a cabinet, next to the others.

"That's not what I meant, and you know it."

Pipette tips scattered as I knocked over a bag. I swept the dirty ones into a cleaning/sterilizing unit. "Speaking of glassware, how do we protect it?"

"We've got padding to wrap around the flasks and beaker. It's in the closet—don't try to change the subject, Jo. I'm worried about you. I don't believe you're taking your mother's death as well as you want me to think you are."

I walked away from him. "So not everyone wails and caterwauls when something bad happens. At least I save the money on tissues."

I dug around in the storage closet until I found several sheets of crumbling foam rubber, probably old enough to be TwenCen. Sometimes Ferdie took reuse to extremes. I bundled them up and turned around.

George was standing right in front of me, arms crossed, his blue-eyed gaze fixing me in place. With most of the equipment already shut down, the lab was unnaturally silent.

We stared at each other for several seconds before George spoke, quietly but with emphasis. "You really are just like your great-grandfather, you know."

I clutched the padding closer to my chest. It was too late; the shot had already gone home. "No, no I'm not." My denial was as flimsy as the padding.

"You are. It's not just your face, or your name, or your wit. You've got the same tough-guy—or tough-girl—pose, but it's all a sham." He paused. "Sometimes I can't help but wonder—"

"Wonder what?" I asked when he didn't finish.

He bent down, his eyes inches from mine. "Sometimes I think you do model yourself after your great-granddad, despite all your talk about not wanting to be like him."

"You don't get me at all, if that's what you think."

"Then why are you on this ship? Why do you want to see him?"

"I don't."

George's eyes widened, and he stepped backward. I took advantage of the distraction to slip past him to stand between benches, shredding the padding.

He shook his head. "Why would you give up a year of your life to travel to another universe and see someone you don't like? It doesn't make sense."

I tried to smile, hoping he didn't hear how fast my heart was beating. He still didn't know why Uncle Jackass had sent me on this mission. "It wasn't much of a life anyway."

"But you wouldn't have left your mom unless you had to."

I stared down at the padding and ripped it up even faster.

George glided over to me and put his hand over mine. "Jo, whatever's going on, I'm on your side. You can trust me. Why can't you tell me, and we'll face it together?"

Would he let me explain everything, or would he think I was as crazy as Jackass and abandon me? I didn't want to risk that.

George sighed. "Does it have something to do with your uncle?"

I looked up at him, then realized that was an answer. Too late, I dropped my gaze. George let the silence build. Finally, when I'd finished shredding the padding, I asked, "What do you know about my uncle?"

"Ferdie got a message from him. He wants us to compare a DNA sample from the other universe with one he provided." His eyes told me nothing about what he was feeling, but I braced myself for the worst. George didn't yell at me, but his voice grew more intense as he asked, "Are you supposed to get a DNA sample from Sean?"

If I spoke, I'd lose control. I nodded instead.

"For what, cloning?" Now, an edge of anger sharpened George's voice. "You can't ask Sean for permission; it's against the travelers' rules. And then you're going to make that clone grow up to be another Sean, no matter what the kid wants? You're the last person I thought would agree to that!"

I dug my nails into my palms. "No!" My voice came out ragged. "I won't let that happen."

"You won't have a choice, Joanna. The travelers won't let you back onboard without the right DNA sample. And once it's out of your hands...."

I glared at George. "If you hate the idea so much, you stop it."

"What do you want me to do, tamper with Sean's DNA? That would be unethical."

"Worse than creating a clone for my uncle?"

His mouth narrowed. "It doesn't matter. The whole project is questionable, and I don't want to be associated with it in any way."

I was surprised by how much that stung me. Did that mean he'd quit seeing me?

"I signed up for this mission to stop my uncle, not help him." Now I straightened up, drawing on my ever-present anger to support me. At least that wouldn't turn against me. "But if that's too unethical for you, then...then...go to hell."

I dashed out of the lab, closer to tears than I'd been in a long time. But I couldn't let them win either.

Perhaps that would be the only victory I'd get.

* * *

We passed through the wormhole that evening. Maybe it was the magnetic shields turned on for the crossing, or maybe it was just lying strapped into my cot, staring at the ceiling with nothing to do but think about my fight with George, but I had a strange dream. I dreamed I was Great-Granddad, playing a family concert in front of Grandpa John, Uncle Jackass and his family, and my parents. Only problem was I'd forgotten how to play the guitar; I couldn't even remember what song I was supposed to sing. I stood there, trying to fake something, until Uncle Jackass called out, "You're not Sean! You're a failure!" They pelted me with anything they could throw.

I woke up to find myself covered in a barrage of clothing and other items I'd forgotten to secure. My sheets stank of sweat.

* * *

"Jo," Lizabeth said to me one evening as I was clearing my lab bench before dinner, "can I talk to you for a second?"

Funny how no one ever asks this when they have something good to say—or when you have a good excuse for refusing. I stalled by placing my beakers one at the time in the dishwasher.

She followed me over. "Look, I know I don't know much about guys, but...."

"But what?"

"Did you and George have a fight lately?"

I cautiously glanced at her. "Did he say something?"

"No, but he didn't have to. It's obvious by the way you two are avoiding each other. Everyone in the lab can tell something's off."

Great. Were they going to kick me out of here? Pluckenreck would be happy if I had more prep time for the mission, but I had enough on my mind these days without thinking about Sean.

Lizabeth dragged a couple of chairs over and claimed one. I climbed into the other, glancing around to make sure the beeps and chimes from the instruments were part of their normal functions, not someone fiddling around with them.

"Do you want to talk about it?" she asked.

I shook my head.

She sighed. "How much do you know about George?"

That was easier. "Well, he likes music, he's sweet and thoughtful, he can be funny—when he's not being stubborn."

"Because you never are."

"Guilty as charged." I spoke lightly, but I could still feel my cheeks grow warm.

"Did George ever tell you why he's on the *Sagan*, not back on Earth?"

"I always thought it was a great honor to be part of this mission."

Lizabeth grinned. "Yeah, I think so too. Who knows, someday we may discover something completely new, not just a copycat universe. That's what I'm staking my Nobel hopes on. But George thinks if we make a major discovery, it would erase the problems he had back at his postdoc lab."

This was something George had never even hinted at. "What problems?"

She bit her lip. "Maybe I shouldn't have said anything, but if you search his records, you'll find it anyway. The professor he was working with took some of George's data for a journal article and altered it without his permission."

I sucked in my breath. "No wonder he's so worried about ethics."

Lizabeth raised a finely arched eyebrow. "You mean your argument wasn't personal? It had something to do with the lab?"

"Not exactly."

She stared at me, the expression in her green eyes neutral. "Then about your mission to clone your ancestor?"

"You know about that?" My voice came out squeaky, making me wince.

"Of course, Jo. All genetic samples come through here, so we get briefed on what to expect."

I worried for a moment if she was going to think I'd purposely lied about mission instead of refusing to talk about it. But she simply shrugged. "Personally, I think it's a waste of time trying to make another Sean Lyon, but if your rich uncle wants to throw a few million credits our way, I'm not going to complain. Why send you, though? You don't seem to care about Sean."

"I don't." I got up to start the dishwasher. "But I'm a victim of Jackass's credits too."

"Ah."

It was hard to read what she meant by that one syllable. Was she indifferent, or disappointed in me? I swallowed and wished I'd never set foot in the genetics lab. Sabotage was easier to contemplate when you didn't know the people who would be affected by your actions.

For a couple of minutes, the only sound in the lab was the dishwasher starting its cycle. Lizabeth put the chairs back and turned off all the equipment not in use. "Well, I hope you and George can work things out. Only a couple more weeks until you visit the other Earth. Are you excited about that, at least?"

I wasn't in the mood to be excited over anything.

After she left, I reviewed George's biography on the *Sagan's* personnel roster, then cross-checked records on the institutions where he'd studied. I did find a reference to a professor being dismissed from a university for falsifying data, but there were no mentions of George in the article. I'd have to wait until the return leg of the trip, when we were closer to Earth, to dig deeper.

Or I could just ask George himself. I gritted my teeth. Why hadn't he told me about this himself, if it was so important to him? But how could I approach him without revealing Lizabeth had shared his secret? And would this make any difference in how he viewed my mission—and me?

My handheld dinged with a message. "Ms. Lyon, please report to the mess hall for a TwenCen presentation."

George and I were going to have to go a little longer without talking to each other, but we were due for a long conversation.

* * *

"Hurry up, Ms. Lyon," Pluckenreck said as she grabbed my arm. Her spectacles slipped off her nose as she tried to pull me towards the shuttle. "We can't miss our launch window."

We'd come as close to the other Earth as we dared. TwenCen tech was puny compared to what we had, but it was still capable of picking up signals from the *Sagan*. A smaller shuttle, though, would have a better chance of approaching the other Earth undetected. All the other travelers were already on board, but I was waiting to see if George would show up. Since our argument, we only talked to each other in the lab, and then only when it was necessary.

It doesn't matter if he comes or not. We had some fun times, but it wasn't anything special. I couldn't even lie to myself; I turned my head as soon as I heard him call my name from the doorway.

"George!" I twisted out of Pluckenreck's grip.

"Ms. Lyon, we have two minutes before they depressurize the shuttle bay," Pluckenreck said.

She intended to hurry me into the shuttle, but I chose to interpret her words as giving me a minute thirty seconds with George. Now I wished we hadn't wasted the time we'd had together earlier. Slipping out of my pumps, I sprinted across the cold metal deck to him. The floor was so smooth that when I tried to stop, I slid into him instead. He caught me, and I put my arms around him. "I'm sorry I swore at you," I whispered into his ear. I didn't have time to pussyfoot around. "Lizabeth told me about that cheating prof of yours. This isn't like that...."

"I know; you were right. I'm sorry for what I said too." He squeezed me tight. "We'll talk about the...project when you return. And mine. Just come back safely. I know you don't like your famous ancestor, but try not to kill him. You'll ruin the travelers' timeline."

I let out a short laugh at that, the first time I'd laughed since I'd heard about Mom.

George and I kissed, but it felt like it hardly started before the computer announced, "One minute to commencement of shuttle bay depressurization. Fifty-nine, fifty-eight...."

As much as I wanted more time with George, I had to leave. No one else was in the shuttle bay. I squeezed him one last time and whispered, "I love you."

"I love you too, Jo." He kissed me again, then released me. "But you'd better hurry!"

I ran as fast as I could without risking a fall. My pumps weren't where I'd left them. Panic flared within me, but I didn't dare stop to look for them. I dashed inside the shuttle with less than thirty seconds left. The door slid shut, cutting off my last glimpse of George. A silent, thin-lipped Pluckenreck glared at me through her glasses, but a few of the other travelers applauded. Winnie waved my pumps over her head; relieved, I dropped into the empty seat next to her.

"Now, remember, travelers," Pluckenreck said, clutching her spectacles as the shuttle accelerated out of the bay and into space. "While you're on alt-Earth, always stay within your assumed identities; in fact, it wouldn't hurt to start using them here." That wouldn't be much of a problem for me; I got to keep my name. "And please remember to be extremely cautious about what you do or say. We're still not sure how this timeline differs from ours, or what a careless slip of the tongue might change."

She continued to lecture us all the way down to alt-Earth, repeating points she'd said in our shipboard classes. After a while, I tuned her out to think about George. Even after that fight, he still loved me? Could we have a future after this trip? How could we make that work when he was stationed on the *Sagan* and I lived on Earth? It would be easier for him to return to Earth than for me to get a permanent position on the spaceship, but I didn't want to ask it of him.

We landed in a cold, dark desert. I didn't have time to appreciate the clean air or the myriad of stars—and the invisible *Sagan*—above us before they brought us underground into what had been an abandoned mining tunnel, now dug out, reinforced, and partitioned into rooms.

Winnie and I, along with half a dozen other female travelers, were shown to a long room with rows of cots where we could sleep until morning. We chatted for a while about our initial impressions, but we didn't have much to discuss yet. Still, I stared at the ceiling for a long time, listening to faint snoring from the woman next to me, as I realized soon I would encounter Sean. Not the world-famous musician my uncle idolized, not the ancestor who'd ignored his first son by his longtime girlfriend and overcompensated with his second son and only wife, but a guy my age who wasn't known outside of a few Chicago clubs. How bizarre to think of him as a human being, not some larger-than-life legend overshadowing everything I was. How was I supposed to tell him off when he hadn't done anything yet and I wasn't supposed to reveal his future? What was he really going to be like?

Suddenly I had a feeling maybe I didn't know as much about Sean as I thought I did.

After breakfast—fresh fruit and real eggs tasted decadent after months of the *Sagan's* supplies—Pluckenreck shoved my luggage, tickets, and purse of money at me, then ushered me into a car along with a few other travelers. We were all silent as we headed for the airport, staring out the windows at the other Earth. The desert gradually gave way to small towns.

"Well, so far, it's not much different from home," I said. A couple of the travelers smiled, but no one seemed inclined to talk.

At the airport, Pluckenreck took each traveler aside to guide them to their gates and give them last-minute advice. She left me until last.

"Now remember, Ms. Lyon; maintain your cover. Don't tell him when you're from. And don't forget," she narrowed her eyes, "that DNA sample is your ticket back onto the *Sagan.* Your uncle doesn't want you returning home without it."

So, George was right; even though Jackass was in another universe, he was still trying to control me. I forced a tight smile. "I understand." If only I understood how to thwart him without stranding myself in this world. "You know, we never went over how I'm supposed to introduce myself to Sean."

She looked scornfully at me. "You're his cousin."

"But why am I meeting him?"

"That's up to the individual traveler to decide."

"How come no one told me that sooner?"

"We covered it at the very first session, the one you missed." She smirked. How could she keep taking that mix-up so personally? "If you don't have a plan by now, Ms. Lyon, you'd better think fast. Good luck."

She turned on her high heels and strode off for the exit. "Fuck you too, bitch," I whispered.

I decided not to worry about meeting Sean for now and focus on catching my flight. I was a little worried about my documents, but the clerk accepted them without question. No one worried about terrorism in these times. I found another surprise at the bottom of my purse: an audiorecorder. Did they expect me to bring back music too? Too bad I couldn't bring Sean himself back for Uncle Jackass; he'd probably hand over all of his credits to hear one note from Sean's lips.

I was too tired to people-watch, so I bought a zine at a kiosk. The paper pages felt flimsy, like they would tear if I touched them, and there was no way to block all the silly ads on every page—the zine was more ads than articles. Even the articles were stupid, full of nothing but advice on men. I looked for something that would help me with George, but there was nothing. Besides, I already knew I had to solve my Lyon problem before tackling my Harrison problem.

I was so tired I slept most of the flight to Chicago, despite the uncomfortable seat. The closer I got to Great-Granddad, the more I wondered if this really was a good idea. It didn't seem right to clone him without his permission, but I couldn't ask for it without giving myself away.

It was mid-afternoon in Chicago when we arrived, windy and much colder than I expected. I stopped into the women's restroom to inspect myself. All the practice wearing skirts and sweaters was paying off; I looked halfway presentable. I straightened my stockings, retied the long pink scarf restraining my hair, and buttoned up my coat. Then I hailed a taxi to take me to Sean Franklin Lyon.

CHAPTER FIVE

As the taxi took me from Midway Airport to Morgan Park, the South Side neighborhood where Sean lived with his grandmother, I gawked at the city like a tourist. This Chicago was much different from the one I knew. Even though this city was younger than mine, the buildings seemed older, built out of brick and steel instead of reinforced plastic and glass. The cars were bigger, noisier, and dirtier. The people seemed odd in their similarity; the men all wore suits, and the women dresses. There wasn't much variety in their skin tones or hairstyles. Ethnic stores and restaurants were hard to spot. Chicago neighborhoods weren't as diverse in this time as they were in mine, so that made sense.

After a while, I leaned back against the patched seat to figure out how to approach Sean. How could I tell him I was a cousin he'd never heard of and make him believe me? Maybe I could pretend I was new to Chicago; I could tell him that I was looking for a job. Or graduate school; I was applying to one of the colleges in Chicago. Which ones were around during the TwenCen? The only one I could think of was the University of Chicago. They still did research there in my time; I hoped they did so now.

We finally arrived in the Morgan Park neighborhood. Despite the cold, children jumped rope or played games on the sidewalk. They eyed me curiously as I stepped out of the cab in front of Sean's house. It looked just like any other one on the block. This neighborhood had been bombed out before I was born, so I'd never seen it. The rose bushes Sean's Grandpa Patrick had planted under the windows were brown in the late fall, but I'd read about how Sean used to play in front of them when he was a boy.

I took a deep breath as I faced the house. Time to see if my unplanned plan would work. I wished I had a letter of introduction or some other way to convince Sean's grandmother I was a relative. All I had to rely on were my looks—and my memory. I hoped I had all my ancestors correctly linked.

I dragged my suitcase over the steps and knocked on the door. As I waited for someone to answer, I wiped my sweaty palms on my coat. Sean's grandmother, his mother's mom, opened the door partway. She looked a little younger than she did in the 2-D pictures I'd seen of her. Her hair was more gray than dark brown. Her plain blue dress did little to accent her features, but even though her mouth was sternly closed, I could see a few faint laugh lines at the corners.

"Good afternoon, Mrs. Murphy." I smiled as politely as I knew how. "I'm Joanna Lyon, Sean's cousin."

Her eyes were flat with distrust. "His cousin?"

"My father was William Lyon, James Lyon's brother." I was pleased I got the lie out smoothly, but my cheeks grew warm.

"I know Jamie." Her voice was cool. Sean's father had joined the Army after getting his wife pregnant, but from what I knew of family history, he'd done so to get out of raising a child instead of to defend his country. Mary Murphy stared at me again. "Where are you from?"

"California. I've come to Chicago for graduate school."

"You sure do look like a Lyon." Now she opened the door enough to let me inside. "Where are you staying? Why don't you come in for a while, and I'll make you something to eat. You must be hungry, traveling all that way."

She led me down a dim hallway to the kitchen. A calendar of saints hung on one wall, and white lace curtains lent dignity to the scratched table and well-used pots. Grandma Mary—she insisted I call her that— gave me a cup of strong tea and a plateful of greasy meat and overcooked potatoes. With the food, the pollution, and the second-hand smoke, this trip was going to cut at least ten years off my life.

Still, I was so hungry even the grease tasted good. I ate as best as I could while answering Grandma Mary's questions about "the family out West."

"And what does your father do?" she asked as I finished my meal.

How do you explain two mediocre albums, a handful of holo appearances, and a share in a celeb PR firm to a TwenCen person? "He's an entertainer," I started to answer. At Grandma Mary's frown, words came to me. "But he's given that up; he never was much good at it. These days he's part owner of a business." Not that he needed to work, with his own share of Great-Granddad's money.

"Well, at least he's respectable, then." Grandma Mary examined my appearance as if she still wasn't sure about me. "Where are you going to school?"

Our heads both turned as something dark flashed by the window, followed by a man at the back door. I clenched my fork as if it were a weapon. Was it Sean, or his grandfather? Judging by the black hair, it had to be Sean. My great-grandfather, as large as life and twice as intimidating. Why had I ever thought meeting him was a good idea?

Grandma Mary pursed her lips as he stepped through the door. I couldn't tell if she disapproved of his outfit—not just a leather jacket, but black leather pants as well—or the cigarette smoke that clung to him. I'd never smelled it before, but it was so foul it couldn't be anything else. How could he tolerate, let alone enjoy, such a filthy habit?

"I just got word of a gig downtown tonight, Grandma." He unzipped his jacket. "It'll run late, so don't wait up."

He didn't even look in my direction as he threw the jacket at my face. I caught it, but the stench made me sneeze. Grandma Mary gasped. "Sean Franklin Lyon, haven't I taught you any decent manners? You don't treat your cousin like that, especially when she's come such a long way!"

"Cousin?" He turned toward me and raised his eyebrows. Frowning, he leaned forward. I knew he was very nearsighted—and too vain to cover his dark blue eyes with thick-framed glasses. "Who are you?"

I let him come a little closer before whipping his jacket at him. Even with his poor vision, he still raised his hands in time to protect his face. *Too bad.* "Call me Jo," I said.

"Jo What?"

"Lyon."

He stood very still. "I hope you're lying about that."

I had to phrase this carefully, or else he'd sense my falsehood. I tilted my face to meet his. "My name really is Lyon, and I share one-eighth of your genes."

Sean and Grandma Mary stared at me with curious faces. I wanted to slap my forehead; how much did the average person of this era know about genetics? Sure, Watson and Crick had figured out the structure of DNA by now, but that didn't mean everyone knew it.

"She's your Uncle Will's daughter, Sean. She's here for school." Grandma Mary reached past Sean to take my plate. "You still didn't say where you were studying, or what. Teaching, maybe, or nursing?"

"Thanks. And I'm not interested in nursing or teaching. I'm going to study genetics at the University of Chicago."

Now the stare of horror from Grandma Mary made me wonder if I'd sprouted another head. "You can't go there, Joanna! That's a bad neighborhood!"

Oops. In my time the university still existed, but it was surrounded by vertical farms, research labs, and housing. Some of the areas were off limits, but it wasn't any more dangerous than anywhere else in the city. "I didn't know that. But I'm sure I can take care of myself."

Sean raised an eyebrow, but I wasn't sure if he was impressed or scornful. "What kind of music do you like, Jobanana?"

Great; he thought I was fruit. If he kept that up, he'd be wearing a banana. Would that change the timeline?

Frowning, Sean asked, "Don't you like music?"

Focus, Jo. Don't let yourself get distracted. Just play along for now. I shrugged. "I listen to all types of music."

"Including rock and roll?"

"It's...all right, I guess."

He scowled, and I suppressed my delight at annoying him. "You've probably never heard anything good. Do you want to come hear me play tonight?"

Uncle Jack had specified I get live cells from Sean to make sure the DNA wasn't degraded. I wouldn't be able to take a sample at the concert, but it would be a good place to use my audiorecorder. And I could piss Sean off even more afterward by insulting his playing—but I'd have to be careful not to make him give up.

"Sure." I smiled, but then I remembered my suitcases. "But I haven't found a place to live yet. I'll have to go downtown anyway and book a hotel—"

"Nonsense." Grandma Mary shook her head. "You can stay with us. Sean, she can have your room." She batted him lightly with a wooden spoon. "And for Heaven's sake, clean up in there. Pigs would be ashamed to call that mess a sty."

"Yes, Grandma." He pitched his voice into falsetto range. "Oh, please, not the spoon! Anything but the spoon!"

I had to bite my tongue to keep from laughing. Sean had a sense of humor, but I didn't want him to think I found him funny. One joke wasn't going to make up for a lifetime of anger.

Sean looked at me, stuck his tongue out, then grabbed my suitcases and left while Grandma Mary told me every horror story she could think of about the neighborhood surrounding the university. I nodded earnestly, as if I meant to take her advice. When she finally let me go to Sean's room, my suitcase lay in the center of the unmade bed. I kicked my way through dirty socks and shirts to stare at the Elvis posters and crate of record albums and 45s. In a few years, teenagers would surround this house, drooling at a chance to see this room, and Grandma Mary would learn to be less trusting of strange girls. But as I stood in Sean's bedroom, not much bigger than my room on the *Sagan*, the thing that impressed me most was how ordinary it seemed. His clothes looked so different from modern ones, and the only personal electronics device he had was a tiny radio, but I could picture Sean in here, strumming away the dreary Chicago winters with his plans to make it big. I thought about myself back on Earth, reading journal articles and dreaming of a Ph.D. Some things, like dreams, transcended history.

Someone knocked on the door. "Hey, Jobanana, if you're coming, let's get going. I need to meet with the band before the show."

"Just a minute," I called back. I considered wearing my red dress, but it reminded me too much of George. Instead, I changed my sweater for a white blouse and ran a comb through my hair. After checking on the recorder, I left the room. Sean had a new shirt on under his jacket, but otherwise he hadn't made any preparations that I could see. He grabbed his guitar case and waved at Grandma Mary, who stood at the kitchen sink, her hands covered in soap bubbles.

"One moment, you two." She dried her hands on a towel. "We should get a picture for the family album while you're all dressed up. Now, where did I put the camera?" She puttered over to the hall closet and peered at the inside. "No, not here. Must be in the bedroom...."

"Grandma, can't it wait?" Sean yelled at her as she disappeared. "We're gonna miss the bus!"

I was no more eager to get my picture taken with him than he was with me, but a couple of minutes later, when she returning brandishing some electronic device as big as my hands, beaming with pleasure, neither of us had the heart to deny her. She gestured at us to stand near the fireplace, then to put our arms over each other's shoulders. I tried not to grimace at touching Sean's jacket. Then we had to force fake smiles while she flashed a bright light at us, not once, but twice.

I knew they didn't have digital cameras in this era, so once I could see again, I asked, "When will the pictures be ready?"

"Oh, I'm not even halfway through this roll yet," Grandma Mary replied. "I'll probably finish it for Christmas, then I have to have it developed."

I should be headed back to my universe by then. It was a little disappointing that I'd never see the picture, but I didn't think it would be a very flattering one, even if it was only 2D.

"Come on, Jobanana." Sean grabbed his guitar. "Looks like we might have to run for it."

He bolted out the door without another word to his grandmother. I waved at her, then followed.

* * *

Sean didn't say much on the bus ride back into downtown Chicago. The sun had already set, but lights illuminated a few office buildings. I was surprised by how much I missed the city I knew: the sleek, sculptured buildings; the speedy monorail system; the variety of restaurants. I wondered what Mom would have thought of this place, and I squeezed my eyelids shut.

"You must really hate Chicago if you can't even bear to look at it in the dark," Sean commented.

I willed my hatred into a laser beam, but when I opened my eyes, he didn't disintegrate. "It's not that."

"Did you leave someone behind?" he asked.

"Yeah," I admitted.

"That's a load of cr—of nonsense. Who'd go for an over-educated girl like you?"

"I don't know, maybe someone a lot smarter than you?"

The bus stopped. Sean rose so quickly a couple of people got between him and me. I hurried to follow him. Once outside on the street corner, Sean lit a cigarette as if it was a guide to our destination.

"Grandma always wanted me to go to school, to make something of myself," he said. Shoving his cancer stick in his mouth, he crossed the street. Most of the stores in this area were already closed, with metal bars blocking their entrances. "I suppose I could have made her happy, but it wouldn't have made me happy being an architect or a dentist." He glanced sideways at me. "I hope she doesn't start nagging me to be more like you. What made you decide to study whatever-it-was again?"

"Genetics. It's the study of how traits are passed along, like height or eye color." Or musical talent, I thought to myself. "As for why I want to study it, well, it helps me understand more about my family."

He let out a sharp laugh. "Are they as messed-up as mine?"

Oh, the stories I could tell him if I could speak freely. Instead, I said, "Your grandmother seems nice enough," in a tone that I hoped would encourage him to talk.

"She's the only one left who gives a—who cares about me." I would have smiled at his change in word choice if he hadn't sounded so bitter. "Everyone says Dad ran off to war so he wouldn't have to take care of me. I stayed with my mom for a while, but when she took up with someone else who didn't want another guy's kid, she gave me to Grandma Mary and moved south. By the time I reconnected with my mom, she already had cancer."

I knew all this, but I hadn't expected him to tell me himself. "I'm sorry" didn't seem like an adequate response, and I didn't think he'd want a touch, even in sympathy. "My parents didn't get along either," I said.

He halted, turning an intense gaze onto me. "Really?"

"Yeah." I was surprised at his fascination for a moment before I remembered most people still got married in this era, and divorce wasn't common. "I never saw much of my dad when I was growing up."

"Huh." His voice was more surprised than angry now. "I guess some things run in families."

I scowled. "You think we're doomed?"

"I don't ever want to get married. Women and kids tie you down." He resumed walking. "Besides, when I'm famous, I'll get all the girls I want."

I said nothing. I knew he'd hold this attitude for about another ten years; he wouldn't marry the mother of his first son, Charlie, no matter how much she pleaded or raged, despite the large settlement he had to give her privately to avoid scandal. But once he toured the Philippines and met Baby, he'd mature into the activist and family man most people remembered him as. Pluckenreck would be furious if I told Sean his future, but I didn't think he'd believe me anyway.

We walked a couple more blocks, passing more storefronts. Soon, they gave way to restaurants and bars. I smelled meatloaf and pie in front of a diner and vomit next to a bar. The next bar seemed classier, with piano music and dressed-up customers. Sean led me two more doors down, to a metal door. The words "White Knight" were scrawled on it. Sean didn't play here very often; I was expecting either the Casablanca or the Jupiter Juniper. Jackass and other fans back home would be elated to hear Sean's performance tonight. As he preceded me down the poorly lit stairwell, I fumbled inside my purse and double-checked my recorder.

A middle-aged man guarded the door at the bottom. "She's with me," Sean said to him.

The guard stared at Sean's guitar case before nodding and letting us pass.

There was nothing noble about the White Knight. Numerous candles cast shadows on the walls. The air was so pungent it should've been classified as a chemical weapon. Despite the poor atmosphere, the tables were already about half full. Most of them were occupied by couples, but some of the ones closest to the stage were home to groups of girls who shrieked and waved at Sean. Maybe he played here more often than I knew.

"Make yourself at home," Sean said. He bounded onto the stage and disappeared behind the curtain.

I managed to find an unoccupied table close enough to the stage for me to make my secret recording. The cramped place filled quickly, with dressed-up girls chattering over the background music—recorded, not live--about their favorite musicians. I didn't recognize most of the names they mentioned, but Sean's came up several times. Young men lined the walls, many of them in leather jackets like the musicians, but younger and with softer faces.

At some signal I didn't notice, all the girls around me whipped hairspray, makeup, and combs out of their purses and preened furiously. Never mind the ozone layer; the hairspray was thick enough to create holes in my lungs. I coughed and fanned myself. As I was wondering if I should pretend to primp too, the girls put their stuff away. The record playing in the background ended, and an older guy all in black with thinning hair stepped onto the stage. "Hi everyone, thanks for coming," he said. "We hope you're enjoying the drinks as much as you'll enjoy tonight's act. Ladies and Gentlemen, Sean Lyon and the Pride!"

Furious applause erupted as the curtain opened. Sean stood off to the side as if he didn't notice the audience. Since he didn't have his glasses on, they were probably all a blur to him, but with the way he tilted his chin and thrust himself forward, he looked too cool to touch. Behind him were another guitarist, a bassist, and a drummer, all in enough black leather to make bovines afraid. I leaned forward, trying to identify them. "Cole Breadmann, Willie Hi-Hat, and Paul Grove," I whispered into the recorder. They'd all played with Sean before, though not always in this configuration. Sean tended to switch his backing musicians around so none of them could challenge him.

A dark-haired girl up front passed glass soda bottles onto the stage. "Thanks, Deborah," Paul, the bassist, said as he set his down. Cole brought one back to Willie, the drummer. Sean raised his guitar to his chest. As one, the four of them broke into "Be-Bop-A-Lula."

I'd heard this song before, of course, on Sean's *Roots of Rock* album. But the sheer energy they put into it astounded me. Despite their primitive equipment, the sound resonated in my bones. Nothing on HitNet had a tenth of this emotion! I couldn't tear my gaze from the tiny stage.

After they finished the song, Sean stepped forward to speak; several of the girls around me sighed. "Good evening, everyone, thanks for coming here tonight. As a special request from Susan, we're going to do 'Twenty Flight Rock!'" He stepped back to play, jerking the neck of his guitar.

As the set continued, Sean dominated the other musicians. Although Paul took lead vocals on a couple of songs, Sean put more of himself into his lyrics. Every reference to rock, every guitar solo, was a musical come-on directed to every single girl in the audience. They fawned over him like he'd already been anointed as the next rock star, leaning forward in their seats, moaning as if they were going to climax right there. Meanwhile, I sat stiffly, arms crossed over my chest. I'm not a prude, but seeing my ancestor as an object of sexual worship made me uncomfortable. I noticed Paul stare at me, then nudge Sean as if daring him to conquer the last stubborn female in the audience. I grinned. There was no way I was going to swoon over my great-grandfather, no matter how exciting his performance was.

Sean drained the rest of his drink. "We're going to slow things down a bit," he said to the audience. "This next number...it's not one we play very often, but my cousin's in the audience tonight, and she made me think of it." He smiled a challenge in my direction as if he could see me without glasses. "Anyway, it goes a little something like this."

Sean settled into his arrogant-seeming performance stance, guitar braced high on his chest, head tilted back, and legs slightly apart. But when he sang, his voice was as poignant as a child's:

You said forever,

You said you'd stay,

This boy trusted you,

Then you went away.

My spine turned to ice. Back in my world, I'd seen some of Sean's handwritten songs, including an early one named "Dad's Song." When Sean was in his thirties, he rewrote it and released it as "Father, Farewell." We had no record of him performing the early version. After hearing the anguish in his voice, I could understand why. Was this what it had felt like to have been abandoned? I remembered the day my dad left my mother, how I'd come home from school to find her slumped over in the kitchen, muttering over and over "What am I going to do?" She didn't even glance at the perfect score I'd gotten on my spelling test. I felt like I'd lost both of them.

Sean's voice rose soulfully for the middle section:

Why did you leave me,

Won't you come back home,

Can't you forgive me,

And never more roam?

It wasn't your fault, I wanted to tell him. It wasn't your fault that your father was too immature to cope with a baby and the doctors didn't find your mother's ovarian cancer in time. But why did I feel I should have done more to protect my own mother?

I feel so guilty,

Even though I was true,

That was how I felt about my mom.

I wish I could see you,

And say, "I love you."

But I couldn't say that to her anymore.

I'd spent my life up to that point hiding from my deepest emotions behind a wall of anger raised the day my parents split. But Sean had honed his own pain into a knife only his voice could wield, and he sliced through my inner barrier as if it didn't exist.

I couldn't keep my tears in any longer; they blended with the sweat on my face. I wiped them off, but I was helpless to stop them.

Silence filled the White Knight for a minute when the song ended. Applause came slowly, as if no one else could appreciate what Sean had done. A scowl flashed over his face before he stepped back and gestured to his band. They ripped into a raucous version of "What'd I Say." It was probably meant to diffuse the emotions Sean had stirred, but for me it wasn't enough.

I rose and pushed my way through the crowded tables. A few girls muttered as I blocked their view. I dashed up the steps leading from the club, past the surprised bouncer, to the street. Leaning against a cold lamppost, I sobbed out all the tears I'd been saving since I was a child.

CHAPTER SIX

I wasn't sure how long I wept before I heard Sean calling, "Jo? Joanna? Where are you?"

I looked toward his voice. All I could see of him was his face and the orange glow from his cigarette. The trails of my tears chilled my face. What if he noticed them? He'd be sure to mock me. I gulped deep breaths of frigid air, trying to regain control. Damn; he homed in on me so quickly I couldn't even find my handkerchief. The best I could do was shake my hair so that it curtained my face.

"What are you doing out here by yourself?" Sean asked as he entered the lighted area. He scowled as if he'd been sent into a snowstorm to round up a naughty child. "This isn't the best neighborhood."

"I'll tell the muggers that if I see any." I winced as I heard myself. I'd tried to sound confident and capable, but my voice came out strained.

He stepped a little closer, and his scowl disappeared. "Are you all right?"

"Fine. Peachy. Whatever you say around here." I sniffed. "Why aren't you on stage?"

"We get a break between sets. I could sure use one after that song." He shook his head. "I forgot what it does to me. What did you think?"

"The slow one? It...it was very sad." Trying to turn his attention away from me, I asked, "What is it about?"

"My dad." He dropped his cigarette stub and ground it out. "My bandmates say no one cares about that kind of stuff, that I should stick to love songs. But I got all these feelings inside me, and they just have to get out."

Why was he telling me this? Had he actually doubted himself? That was something left out of the biographies. But was I supposed to encourage him? Was that interfering with the way his life was supposed to develop?

Sean stared at me as if waiting for a response, then snorted. "I guess a square like you wouldn't understand. But I thought...."

It shouldn't have stung as much as it did; maybe he'd flayed all of my emotions raw. But I couldn't let that challenge pass unanswered. I raised my head slowly and shook my hair away. "Your song...it made me think of my mom."

Something somber flickered in his eyes. "Your mother?"

"Yeah. She's been ill for a long time. I didn't want to leave her alone and come here, but I had to. Then I found out she...she died." Fresh tears sprung up from the inexhaustible well inside of me. I wanted to wipe them away, but I didn't want to draw attention to them.

Sean touched a rough finger to my damp cheek. "Go ahead, cry for both of us." His voice had an odd note in it. "I lost my mother too."

He pulled me to him. I leaned on his shoulder, put my face on his sweat-soaked leather jacket, and washed it with my tears. He held me awkwardly, as if he didn't console others often, but I didn't mind. I knew he had a hard time showing his own emotions at this point in his life, but I also knew he shared mine. And at least for those few moments, the similarity was a comfort, not a bother.

"Feeling better?" he asked after I stopped.

"Yeah," I answered. I felt exhausted but also relieved, like I'd put down a heavy burden. I fumbled around in my purse for a handkerchief.

"We've got to go back in there, you know. I've got another set to do." He wiped a tear track roughly with his thumb. "And you've got to get on with your own life. Think you're up to it?"

I shrugged. "Don't have much choice, do I?"

"The way I see it, you have two choices, you can live or die." He spat in the street. "Me, I'm going to live, no matter what my parents did to me."

He turned, put his hands in his pockets, and sauntered back to the club entrance. I watched him disappear below the street, annoyed with him. Maybe we'd shared a couple moments of sympathy, but he'd returned to his macho, tough guy pose pretty fast. And thanks to him, I'd never be able to trust my own armor of anger again. Now that I'd cried once, it'd be much easier to do it some other time.

But Sean was right about one thing; protected or vulnerable, I had to get on with my life. And right now, that meant dealing with Sean long enough to steal his DNA so I could return home. I followed him downstairs for the second half of the show.

* * *

I bought myself a cup of coffee to warm up. Someone had taken my seat, so I stood in back and listened to the second set. It went much like the first, except Sean was even rowdier, as if he were compensating for his sympathy for me during the break. He jumped around the stage, traded insults with the other musicians, and swore a blue streak when the amps died during a Buddy Holly cover. Cole jury-rigged the amps back to life, and they closed with a wild version of "Shout," with everyone sharing vocals. They stretched it out to nearly ten minutes and got the audience to join them.

I didn't know what to do once the show was over, so I hung around by the stage while Sean and the others put their instruments away. Several other girls waited with me; I discovered they were Cole's, Willie's, and

Paul's girlfriends. "We're going to check out another group playing at a bar near Wrigley," Paul's girlfriend said. "Are you and Sean coming?"

I looked at him, willing to go along with what he wanted. But after staring at me for a minute, he shrugged. "Maybe not tonight. I better get my cousin home before my grandma complains I'm corrupting her."

The others teased him a bit, but he ignored them. I have to admit I was glad to go back. Between the traveling, the show, and my breakdown, I was drained enough to sleep for a week. I nearly nodded off on the bus, but walking to Sean's house from the bus stop revived me a bit, enough to wonder when I should take the DNA sample. The house was dark; Grandma Mary must have been in bed. Good; one less witness. But could I outlast Sean? He still looked lively enough to dance a jig.

Sean let us into the kitchen and turned on a light. In the still, dark room, he seemed a menacing figure in his black outfit. I was suddenly conscious of being alone with him. He'd already breached my defenses once tonight; God knew what else he would do to mess up my mind.

I bundled up my overcoat and purse in my arms. "Thanks for taking me to your show," I said. "It was really great."

"I know," he said. "The four of us work well together, and people aren't complaining too much anymore when I slip in my own songs." He grinned. "Now all I need to do is find a record company that likes them too."

"I'm sure you will someday." I tried to make it sound like casual encouragement, not prophecy. I mimed a yawn. "Now, good night." I started to leave.

"Are you really that tired? It's still early."

I turned around and gave him my best are-you-kidding stare. "Not all of us are night owls, Sean. You won't believe how far I've traveled today."

"So? Do you have somewhere you have to be tomorrow?" He leered at me. "Or are you afraid I lured you back here under false pretenses?"

Oh, please. I raised my knee. "You try anything, Sean Franklin Lyon, and you'll be singing in a higher register at your next show."

"You wouldn't!"

As tempting as it was, I couldn't, not with my family's future in this universe at stake. But he didn't have to know that. "Are you sure you want to risk it?"

He chuckled. "I like feisty women, but not when they're related to me. God knows I have enough of that with my Grandma." His expression grew solemn. "I just wanted to have a talk. It's not every day I meet someone with parents as messed up as mine."

If he only knew.

Sean filled a kettle with water and placed it in a ring of flame on the gas stove. Then we sat down at the table. He leaned forward, peering at me as if he had trouble seeing me even at this short distance. "So, wanna talk about them?"

I took a deep breath, then told him a carefully edited version of my life. The words came easier than I thought they would. Perhaps that was because Sean wasn't mocking me the way I'd expected him to. He listened closely, occasionally adding his own anecdotes. There were a few times when tears welled in my eyes again, but even though he watched me, I wiped them away and continued with my story. At one point he brought me some strong Irish tea, and it was comforting to hold the steaming mug between my hands.

"Well, at least this is a good place to make a new start," Sean said when I'd finished. "What did you say you were going to study again?"

I decided to be more general this time. "Science."

"So you can become a nurse?"

"No, I want to do research."

"Like Einstein?" Sean snorted weakly, as if he were losing energy. "You don't look much like him."

"What's that supposed to mean?" Irritation chased away my own fatigue. "Women can be scientists too." I had to stop myself before I added "even in your time." "Look at Marie Curie. She and her husband isolated radium from pitchblende. She won two Nobel prizes for her work. And Rosalind Franklin, she's my favorite. I bet you never heard of her, but she managed to take some pictures of DNA that helped Watson and Crick figure out how it was put together."

"DNA? What's that? Desperately Needing Amour?"

"Not quite. DNA stands for deoxyribonucleic acid. It's the stuff our genes are made of, the stuff that makes us us." The stuff that made me so much like him.

He yawned. "Sounds dull, science. All test tubes and white coats and regular routine jobs. There's no art in it."

"Oh, yes there is." I set my cup down and leaned forward. "Yeah, sometimes it does get dull, running the same experiment over and over, looking for the answer you want. Most of the time you can't tell for sure, so you have to change the design of your experiment. Sometimes the experiment works out completely opposite from what you predicted; then you have to change your working theory. But sometimes you get a result that actually tells you something, something that takes you a little farther than you were before, or joins two things you thought were unrelated. That's the joy in science. And science itself is an art, just like your guitar playing. I had to practice the techniques over and over until I got good at them, and I'm always trying to learn new ones. And then you have to learn how to work with other scientists too, so your combined efforts make sense, not a bunch of noise…." I realized I'd gone on too long. "Anyway, maybe you don't see much beauty in science, but if you knew as much about it as I do, you would."

Sean stared at me, eyes wide, for what felt like a long time. One hand crept towards the pocket of his jacket, as if he wanted a cigarette, but he jerked it back. "Maybe you're not so much like me after all," he said finally.

Maybe you're not so much like me… it was like hearing the key open the lock of my prison door. I'd told George I was different from Sean, but I hadn't been sure. But now, after having experienced him and his world, I knew I wasn't him. Hearing it directly from Sean, from an unkempt, shortsighted, witty, and dominating Sean, still smelling of smoke and sweat, weariness showing on his face, confirmed it. No matter how many times people had compared me to Sean before, or how many times they would do it for the rest of my life, I would know the truth. And the truth would set me free.

"I'm not you." I grinned as I looked Sean in the eyes. "I'm not you."

He frowned. "Well, you needn't sound so pleased about it."

I couldn't help it; I laughed. "Never mind," I said as he raised his eyebrows. "It's a personal matter."

We finished our tea and talked about everything: books, music, and the differences between California and Chicago. He was an excellent conversationalist; if he didn't have something intelligent to say about a topic, he'd crack a joke. I had a hard time keeping up with him, especially since I didn't want to talk about things that didn't exist yet and didn't know much about California in this time period.

Sean seemed more open and friendly during our talk than he had before. I wanted to confide in him, tell him who I really was and what I was doing here. But I didn't dare. For one thing, he might not have believed me, and if he did, I couldn't believe he'd agree to let me sample his DNA. Everything I knew about him suggested he wouldn't like the idea of being cloned. Sean changed his mind more often than he did his clothes, but on something like this I couldn't expect him to agree at any time. Odds were, he'd only get furious at me and kick me out, leaving me stranded here.

Our conversation slowed. I pushed my exhausted brain cells to the limit, trying to think of a way I could feel out Sean's opinions on a procedure that for him existed only in science fiction. Suddenly I realized he was breathing heavily. "Sean?"

He was slumped forward, head resting against his arm, lips slightly open as he blew air through them. He'd taken off his leather jacket; maybe that's why he seemed younger than he really was.

Even legends of rock and roll have to sleep sometime.

I couldn't believe I'd outlasted him. This would be my best chance to sample him without his knowledge—assuming he didn't wake up. I watched him for several moments to make sure he didn't. I tried to think of other alternatives to this—sampling someone else, or even doing a little genetic surgery on my own DNA to pass it off as his. But I didn't have the equipment to do that. More importantly, it was just as unethical to falsify a sample as it was to take it without his permission. I'd known all along I'd have to do this; I might as well get the dirty deed over with.

I pulled a sampler out of my purse, then rose and approached him. "Forgive me," I whispered. "You're still unique no matter how many copies my uncle wants."

He slept on, offering me no absolution.

I clicked the sampler open, exposing the tip. I gently pried Sean's lips apart with one hand and ran the tip over the lining of his mouth. There were plenty of freshly-shed cells there. Some of the cells would still be alive and proliferate in the human-cell-specific medium stored in the sampler. For good measure, I opened the other end of the sample, which contained a preservative, and collected more cells. I covered both ends to prevent contamination, then opened a slit in the center for airflow.

Sean didn't feel a thing.

I contemplated the sampler, admiring its microscopic contents. The cells I had just gathered contained forty-six chromosomes in twenty-three pairs. If I took all the chromosomes from just one cell and carefully laid them end to end, they'd stretch out to about two meters, a little longer than Sean himself. But evolution had packaged the DNA so neatly it all fit in a space just a millionth of a meter across. And in the approximately 30,000 genes encoded in all this DNA were instructions for making one human Caucasian male, thin, black-haired and blue-eyed, with a long nose, bad eyesight, and musical and linguistic gifts.

Who says there's no poetry in science?

I collected a second sample as a backup, then labeled both samplers with Sean's name, my own, and the date. All I had to do now was make sure they were kept at room temperature and received adequate airflow. And turn them over to Pluckenreck so my uncle could create a clone to exploit. I grimaced at the thought.

I hid the samplers back in my purse, then shook Sean. "Sean, Sean, wake up! Wake up and go to bed."

When I did rouse him, he was too tired to appreciate the joke. I helped him make his way over to the sofa, where Grandma Mary had laid out a blanket, pillow, and a change of clothes for him. He lay down, still fully clothed. "Don't I get a goodnight kiss?" he mumbled as I tucked him in.

I kissed his cheek. "Goodnight, Sean."

"G'night…cousin." He was soon asleep again.

I crept upstairs and washed up as quietly as I could. I thought I would have trouble falling asleep, but I think I slept as soon as I excavated the bed and fell into it.

I did have an odd dream, though. Sean and I were back at the White Knight, alone. I sat in the front row, so close I could kick the stage, and Sean sat on the edge, feet dangling over as he strummed his guitar. "Jo, Jo, something to do before you go," he chanted.

I woke late and lay there for a while, staring at the sunlight coming through the window. Sean had given me several gifts last night: the gift of tears, the gift of my own identity, and of course, the gift of his DNA. Though he hadn't meant to give them to me, I still owed him a debt. I could think of only one thing that could equal what he had given me: a chance to escape his murderer in nineteen years.

CHAPTER SEVEN

As I washed myself and got dressed, I tried to figure out how to steer my great-granddad away from the fate he'd suffered in my universe. Unlike Eliot's Prufrock or my nemesis Pluckenreck, I dared disturb the universe; there was no reason to expect this universe to follow mine. But assuming it did and Sean's life here was identical to the one I'd memorized, how could I save him from a fate years away without messing up the rest of his life? Maybe I could warn Sean about his possible fate but emphasize it might not happen. But I couldn't tell him now. Even if he believed me, it seemed cruel. Better to let him live his life normally as long as possible. I'd have to write him a message and put it in a time capsule or something similar. I couldn't leave it in the house; Grandma Mary might find it when she cleaned.

Someone knocked on the door. "Are you up yet, Jobanana?" Sean called. "I want a new shirt."

I threw the rest of my clothing in my suitcase, then opened the door. "The room's all yours."

Grandma Mary was preparing oatmeal for breakfast. She refused my offer to help, so I drifted back into the living room and stared at Sean's guitar, sitting in one of the chairs as if it was another member of this household. I had no reason to stay here anymore; I could make some excuse after breakfast and leave forever. The idea saddened me more than I'd thought it would. But George waited for me back on the *Sagan*, and I needed to make things right with him. Plus now that I had what Uncle Jackass wanted, I had to figure out how to deny it to him.

Sean joined me while I was still contemplating his guitar. "Thinking of dropping your science and taking up music?" he asked in a half-mocking tone.

I shuddered; I hadn't told him about the concert tour I'd escaped from. "It's not for me."

"Of course not." A sly gleam in his eyes contradicted his agreeable tone. "A girl like you wouldn't know the first thing about playing anyway."

I clenched and unclenched my hands at his challenge. Damn it, it was as if he and Uncle Jackass had conspired to goad me into playing again. Part of me wanted to ignore the gibe, but another part wanted to show Sean up. Could I do it? Though he was a passionate guitarist, he wasn't the most technically brilliant one. I knew I'd never match Sean at the height of his touring years, but maybe at this age we had similar experience.

With a smirk, Sean snatched his guitar and strummed the opening to one of the songs he'd played last night. His long fingers glided over the strings. No, I wasn't going to match him, but I could show him that he'd underestimated me.

I reached for his instrument. "May I try?"

He raised his eyebrows in surprise. "You know how?"

"A bit." Even if I'd wanted to reveal my past experience with the guitar, I don't think I could have told him; my mouth was drier than the strings.

"All right, then."

He helped me settle the guitar into place, then stood back and crossed his arms. I wasn't sure if he was worried I was going to damage his precious instrument or just waiting for me to fail so he could laugh.

I gripped the guitar as if trying to hold on to my sense of self. Images blurred through my memory: practicing in front of my cousins and uncle, enduring their insults; the endless parade of performances, each one more terrifying than the previous one. Why was I doing this? I could just hand the guitar over to Sean and walk away, and no one from my world would ever know I'd chickened out. But I would. This song wouldn't be for Uncle Jackass or George or even Sean; it would just be for me.

I closed my eyes and felt my way through "Be-Bop-A-Lula." Sean prompted me when I forgot which chord came next.

"Not bad," he said in a grudging tone. "Here, let me show you a thing or two."

He guided my hands into position for a few chords, and we went over the song again. This time it went a little easier. I played it one more time, a little faster. Sean sang along while tapping the beat with his foot. Our music filled the room, connecting us on a level beyond that of our common blood.

When the song was over, I gave the guitar back to him. My fingertips were raw, but I felt exhilarated. "Thanks," I said. "I'm glad to see I'm not as rusty as I thought." I still never wanted to play in public again, but maybe just for myself or for good friends. All right, mostly for George. The important thing was I didn't have to reject everything Sean had done to separate myself from him.

"You've got some talent," he said. "If they ever let you out of the lab, you should come visit me and my band. We could teach you some tricks."

I couldn't help asking, "Are you saying I should audition?"

"Lord, no." He looked taken aback. "I can't possibly have a girl on the stage with me. How could I score with the fans?"

I wanted to smack him for his sexist attitude, even though I knew he'd drop it when he met my great-grandmother, Baby. Revenge would have to wait.

Grandma Mary called us to the kitchen for oatmeal with lots of butter, bread with jam, and coffee. Sean brought in the newspaper and spread it over the white tablecloth as if we all had to read it at the same time. Everything tasted rich; I had a second helping even though I was sure I'd already put on five kilos from this trip. When I was done, I leaned back with my coffee, savoring the quiet sense of belonging. But did I really? Every glance at the kitchen, with oddly shaped appliances, religious decorations, and food I didn't recognize, reminded me this wasn't my era. It was time to go home, and I had to make up an excuse to leave.

I glanced at Sean's paper, and one of the column headings caught my eye. "Rooms to Let," I said. "May I see that?"

Sean slid the page over without looking up.

I made a show of scanning the listings. "This one looks promising." I pointed to one at random. "Do you mind if I call them?"

"Of course not, Joanna, but you needn't be in such a rush to leave us," Grandma Mary said. "You can stay here as long as you like."

I felt a rush of warmth—and guilt. "Thanks, Grandma Mary. It's nice of you to offer, but it wouldn't work out."

Her fallen expression made me feel even worse. Sean glanced up long enough to say, "She needs to be closer to school, Grandma."

She nodded, though she still didn't look convinced.

Despite my lessons on board the *Sagan*, I didn't feel comfortable using TwenCen phones, so I positioned myself so Sean and his grandmother couldn't see me pretend to dial the numbers. I felt silly trying asking questions of no one. It didn't help when Grandma Mary started offering advice like, "Ask what kind of furnishings it has," and Sean countered with "Ask if it comes with a free elephant." When I finally hung up, the phone was smudged. Ink from the newspaper? I tried rubbing it off, then I had to wash my hands to clean them too.

"They said I could come look at it right away," I told my relatives. "I may as well bring my suitcase."

"Is that it? Where's the rest of your stuff?"

"I'll have it shipped out later."

"All right." She collected the empty dishes. "Will you be back for dinner?"

I sighed. "Probably not."

"Well, if it doesn't work out, the offer still stands. I hope it's in a good part of town! Let us know, will you?" She hugged me before returning to the sink. "Sean, help her with her things, that's a good lad."

I didn't mind that Sean's sexist attitudes required him to carry my suitcase, despite his crack about how I'd packed bricks instead of clothes. The day was cloudy and chilly, with a wind strong enough to make conversation difficult. I tried not to study the neighborhood too much as we walked, even though I knew it would be the last time I saw it. This was supposed to be a casual parting, even if it was final.

Sean dropped my suitcase as soon as we reached the shelter. "Lucky you, moving out," he said. "I can hardly wait until I can be on my own."

"Your grandmother seems nice," I said.

"Yeah, but she's always telling me what to do." He gave me a sharp glance. "Hey, maybe when you're settled, I can drop by."

"There's a roommate," I improvised. "Two, even."

"I hope they're good-looking."

"I think you have plenty of girls chasing after you already."

He grinned at that.

The bus turned the corner. Soon, I'd never see him again. Why was I more disappointed than relieved?

As the bus slowed, I turned and hugged him. "Thanks, Sean."

Still in my grip, he shrugged. "For what?"

"For...everything."

Sean took charge of my suitcase while I searched through my purse for the fare. When I was set, I boarded the bus and paid as smoothly as if I'd been born into this time. I sat by the window so I could watch him walk away. Instead, he stood there and stared at me, as if he suspected this was a final parting. Suddenly, he ran his fingers through his dark hair, making it stick up in all directions. Then he made circles around his eyes with his fingers. What the hell was he doing? It took me a few seconds to figure out he was probably imitating Einstein. Yeah, I really had a chance at matching that genius; our family just had the madness. Still, I couldn't help grinning as we pulled away.

* * *

Now that I no longer had to deal with Sean, I could think about how to thwart my uncle. I turned over ideas in my mind. Someone in the genetics lab would probably compare my sample to Jackass's own DNA. I didn't have any way to alter the sample, and I had to hand it over if I wanted to see George ever again. But he'd already said he wasn't willing to help me alter the DNA. How was I going to stop my uncle from creating a child from Sean Lyon's genes?

I could see two possible futures for the child. In one, the clone would be raised on a steady diet of Lyonism, much as I had been. He'd be trained on guitar, piano, and voice, only he'd be pushed harder than I, a mere girl, had been. Every scribble or doodle of his would be scrutinized for signs of Sean's humor. Every day, he'd have Sean held up before him as an example of greatness; Sean's faults would be downplayed, even made into virtues. I knew from my own childhood what that would be like, and I wouldn't go through it again for all the millions Uncle Jackass had squirreled away.

The second alternative was even worse. Uncle Jackass and the suits at World Music had to know Sean's genius was as much a product of his environment as his genes. If they wanted a second Sean Lyon, they'd have to recreate the original Sean's environment. How far would they go with that? Would they give the child fake parents instructed to abandon him? When the boy was a teenager, would they let him resume a relationship with his mother, then have her pretend to get cancer and die?

I shuddered. They might very well do that.

No matter which scenario played out, this boy was doomed to an unhappy childhood. I knew what it was like being Sean Lyon's great-granddaughter; it would be infinitely worse to be his clone, much worse than what Grandpa John and Great-Uncle Charles had endured. He'd never have a life of his own or be encouraged to develop as a normal child. No one would ever see him as a unique person; they'd always see him as Sean Lyon's clone.…

Unless they'd been through a similar hell.

For this boy to have any chance at all, I'd have to become his mother.

CHAPTER EIGHT

I'd never given motherhood much thought before that moment. Why would I, when I was so busy with work and my too-little time for graduate school? I had no siblings, and my cousins were older than me. All I had to go on about kids was my own childhood, something I tried to put behind me. Weren't kids loud, messy, and expensive? Why would I saddle myself with one when I didn't have to? Uncle Jackass was more than willing to raise a kid; let him have all the headaches. Then I reminded myself who would suffer if my uncle got what he wanted, and it wasn't going to be him. Jackass would pay someone to change the kid's diapers; he'd just show up to brainwash the boy. At least if I was the mother, I could provide some necessary re-education—if I could keep the child. Knowing my uncle, he'd probably try to rip the boy out of me, chewing through the umbilical cord himself if he had to. I clamped my own teeth together. No; I couldn't let that happen. But how could I stop him?

As much as I wanted to see George, I needed to think about this newest problem before I returned to the *Sagan* and surrendered Sean's DNA. So I got off the bus and wandered around downtown for a while. The streets, while not deserted, felt sparser than I'd expected. Many stores were closed. As I passed a drugstore that happened to be open, I remembered my resolution to leave Sean a warning. I went in and bought a pen and stationery with hearts printed on it. It didn't suit either of us, but it was the least offensive pattern I could find. Then I found a deli and ordered lunch. The tuna salad was flavorful, but the coffee was weaker than what I was used to; it took two and a half cups before I finally figured out what to say:

November 5, 1961

Dear Sean,

Thanks for the hospitality last night. I hope you and Grandma Mary didn't waste too much time worrying about me after I left. Are you reading this in 1980? Are you world-famous by now? Did you and your wife Baby inspire a revolution in the Philippines and have a son named John? If you did, then your life paralleled that of my own great-granddad closely enough that I have to warn you of something. But first, I have to explain who I am and where I come from.

As you've probably guessed, I'm not your cousin, I'm not from California, and while I do want to study genetics, I didn't come to Chicago for graduate school. I'm the great-granddaughter of a Sean Franklin Lyon from another universe. It's a weird property of physics that every time there's a choice to be made, the universe splits. This happens all the time, so there are innumerable universes existing alongside our own. I can't explain this too well; I'm not a quantum physicist. People know more about alternate universes in my time than they do in yours, but I think you should still be able to find some information. You can always read some science fiction; it doesn't all come true in my time, but a surprising amount does.

I'm telling you all this because I don't want you to die the way my ancestor did in my universe. Please keep in mind, Great-Granddad, that IT DOES NOT HAVE TO BE THIS WAY. For all I know, it won't happen to you at all; this universe may be different enough to ensure that it won't. But not even I can predict your future; this is just one possible future, one I hope you can avoid.

On December 6, 1980, you and Great-Grandma perform a charity concert at a local venue. Among the fans in the audience is Joseph Balani, a Filipino exile working as a security guard at the Museum of Science and Industry. As you're leaving the stage, he rushes up and stabs you in the chest. You don't make it to the hospital in time.

I had to pause. When I was a child, it'd been awful enough learning about Sean's murder, but he'd been more of a family myth than a real person to me. Now that I'd met him, it felt even worse. Just putting the words down on paper was a battle; I knew I wouldn't have been able to tell him face-to-face, even if he'd listened. But this was the only way to make sure it wouldn't happen here. I drained my coffee, then continued,

I can't tell you how to cheat death—I'm sure you and Great-Grandma can think of something. But please take this warning seriously. Balani blames you for his political exile. He doesn't hurt just you; he screws up the life of every Lyon after you. You don't know what it's like to grow up as one of your descendants. Because you died so young in my universe, we're expected to replace you. And that's impossible. I used to hate you...

I wondered if I should cross that last part out or start over. At one point, I'd wanted to scream those words at him, but I no longer had the heart to. Then I thought about him and smiled. He of all people would understand.

I have more musical talent than my cousins, so my dad's family pressured me to become a musician. But I'm not as gifted as you, and it's not my passion the way genetics is. They tried to make me tour, but it didn't work out. Meeting the real you, not some mythological figure, helped me come to terms with my family—and myself. I know people will always compare me to you, but it's not going to bother me so much anymore. No matter what they want from me, I'm going to live my own life. I hope your life is a long and happy one, and that you get to spend more time with Great-Grandma and Granddad John. Maybe you'll even live long enough to see "my" birth. To quote from one of your best-known songs, knowing isn't everything, but sometimes it's the only thing.

Love from your alternate great-granddaughter,

Joanna Lyon

I placed the letter in an envelope, sealed it, and wrote "For Sean—Do not open until December 1, 1980" on the front of the envelope. That would give him a few days to back out of the concert or hire more bodyguards; I hoped it was enough.

Now, how to make sure he'd get the letter at the right time? For that, I'd have to trust my great-grandmother. I stuffed Sean's letter inside another envelope, then wrote a short note: "Baby, Please hold onto this letter until the right time. It will bring you good luck. Love, An Admirer." From what I knew of her, she was superstitious enough to believe that. I wrote down as much as I remembered of her snail mail address and hoped a post office would help me later with the rest.

I tucked the letter in my purse, then checked the envelope for my plane tickets back to the base. It was empty. How had I lost them? I dumped the purse out on the table and checked every pocket, but I couldn't find anything. For a black moment, I wondered if Pluckenreck had been so eager to get rid of me that she hadn't bothered providing me with a way back. But then my uncle would never get his priceless DNA sample. I examined the ticket envelope again and found a phone number. Relief flooded through me, only to change to irritation when Pluckenreck refused to believe I had the sample.

"It doesn't matter how strange you find the TwenCen, Ms. Lyon." I could hear a sneer in her voice. "You're here until you fulfill your mission."

"I did." I wished I had a handheld so I could send her proof. This antique telephone was so limited.

"You didn't even have a plan to meet Sean," she accused me. "You can't be done already."

"You don't think we Lyons are smart enough to work fast?"

Silence on the other end, followed by a huff. "I'll believe it when I see it. Take the Greyhound bus back to Phoenix, then call me again. If you're wasting my time...."

I hung up before she could finish.

It didn't take me long to realize she'd directed me to the bus to punish me. The nightmare lasted four days—four days of bumpy roads, greasy meals, and awkward attempts to clean myself in dirty restrooms. The only good thing about it was I was able to find a post office, ask the clerk how to send a letter to the Philippines, and mail Baby's letter during one of the stops. When I called Pluckenreck after arriving in Phoenix, she humphed at me, told me to wait there, and disconnected. She showed up an hour later in a contemporary car. Pluckenreck rolled down the window and stuck out her hand. "Let me see the sample."

I didn't give it to her—I had a sudden flash of her snatching it and abandoning me—but I held it so she could see the label. She sighed. "Get in. They can test it at the base."

Relieved, I crept into the seat next to her.

She drove us out of the city, into a desert that seemed to go on forever. Neither of us spoke to the other on the trip. When we arrived back at the mining camp, she took us underground and led me straight to a lab even smaller than the one on the *Sagan*. For a brief moment, I wondered if George had transferred down here and what I'd say to him. But I didn't recognize the technician scanning sample pens.

"Give it to him," Pluckenreck told me.

Repressing a sigh, I handed over one of the DNA-filled samplers and hoped it was the right thing to do.

"Could I have the rest of the samplers?" he asked me. "If they haven't been used, we can give them to other travelers."

Keeping my expression as neutral as I could, I dug two pristine samplers out of my purse. Had anyone kept track of how many samplers I'd been given? Could I pretend I'd lost the other one?

"That's only three," Pluckenreck said. "Where's the other one?"

I felt my face flush and knew I wouldn't get away with a lie. I couldn't even look the tech in the eyes after retrieving the final sampler, the one with Sean's DNA. I could imagine Sean scowling at me and wanted to apologize again.

The tech nodded at me. "It'll be a few hours before the results are ready. You can grab some lunch in the mess hall or relax in the rec room."

"Is there someplace I can borrow a handheld?" I asked. "Or are we not allowed them down here?"

"There are a couple of entertainment handhelds in the rec room, but they're offline."

I'd been hoping to contact George, but I thanked him anyway.

I showered and changed into my cleanest set of TwenCen clothes, then headed for the mess hall. The meatloaf was lukewarm and salty, but since meat was more common on this Earth than mine, I paid attention to every bite. As I considered dessert, another traveler from my classes came in. He wore a suit and tie similar to those I'd seen men wearing in Chicago. I wondered if he still had to leave on his mission or if he'd already completed his, like me.

He passed by my table on the way to the buffet. "Do you know when the next shuttle leaves?" I asked.

"They only run at night," he replied. "But I don't know if the wormhole storm threw off the schedule, or if they'll be pulling us all out of here."

I sat up straight. "The wormhole storm?"

"Yes. It happened a few days ago. All sorts of exotic particles spewed out of the wormhole, and it even shrank."

I crumpled my napkin. "Was the ship damaged?"

"It's fine. They raised their shields in time. They say the planet isn't in any danger either. But the physicists are still trying to figure out what it means, if anything."

"Why? Is this something new?"

He nodded. I thought back to my letter. Had I really done something that would change history? But Sean hadn't read it yet; it was still on the way to Baby. I couldn't have possibly disturbed the universe.

Pluckenreck returned. "There you are, Ms. Lyon. Come to my office. I want a full report on your trip."

She didn't get one. Oh, sure, I told her about Grandma Mary and the concert. I sang one of Sean's songs for her; she tapped her foot in time with the beat, but she didn't crack a smile. I even described taking the DNA sample. But I left out my outburst at the concert and the letter I mailed to Baby. She still didn't seem satisfied.

"And you're sure you didn't tell him about his future?" she asked over and over. "Not his success, not his murder?"

"Of course not," I said. I willed myself not to flush.

She watched me for a couple of seconds, her eyebrows drawn together skeptically. "And you didn't notice anything out of the ordinary?"

"Compared to our world, all of it was."

She narrowed her eyes. "I don't know if you've heard yet, but there was some unusual activity associated with the wormhole. I just want to make sure the travelers didn't have anything to do with it."

I played dumb. "How could they do that?"

"By changing the history of this planet."

"But aren't we already affecting events just by being here?"

"Not on a scale that affects the wormhole." She sighed and pushed her glasses into place. "And I want to keep it that way."

I stared at her while her words sank in. If I really had changed the wormhole, were we stuck here? And she was going to get us unstuck by letting Sean get murdered? I wanted to protest, but she stared at me so coldly I knew I'd incriminate myself if I spoke.

Her TwenCen phone rang. She turned away from me as she identified herself, then listened to the person on the other end. Sweat gathered in my armpits. When she finished her call, she regarded me for a few seconds before saying, "They've verified your DNA sample is from the test subject. You can take tonight's shuttle back to the *Sagan*. Until then, you're free to wander around the base." The expression in her pale eyes finally warmed. "Well done, Ms. Lyon."

As relieved as I was to escape, I didn't feel I'd done a good job at all.

* * *

With trepidation, I watched the *Sagan* grow larger in the shuttle's overhead holoprojector. Would George be willing to help me wrest control of the clone from Uncle Jackass, or would he despise me for completing my mission? Would he even want to talk to me again? If he didn't, what about Ferdie, Liz, and Livia? It would be a long, dull trip back to my universe if they banned me from the genetics lab.

The docking and repressurizing of the shuttle bay seemed to stretch out another month. At least there were only a few other passengers, so I was able to get off quickly. I scanned the shuttle bay for George, but he wasn't there. Of course he wouldn't have known when I was coming back. Still, all my energy drained out of me, and I trudged to my cabin. Maybe after a proper shower and a good night's sleep on a firmfoam mattress, I'd feel up to facing him.

George waited in front of my door. I could see faint red indentations on his face from his safety glasses. He looked up from his handheld, and a smile lit up his face. Joy chased away my fatigue.

"Your name was on the passenger list," he said, "but I wasn't sure...."

I hesitated for a moment, not wanting to appear too eager, but when he approached me, I dropped the pretense and ran into his embrace. Our lips found each other as if they'd been magnetized.

We finally had to come up for air. George cupped his hand under my chin and gazed at me. "You…you look different," he said.

"Must be the TwenCen dirt. I can still smell cigarette smoke in my hair."

He shook his head. "That's not it. You don't look so angry at the whole world anymore." His mouth quirked. "So, did you kill your great-granddad or make peace with him?"

I let out a rueful laugh. "I came close to changing history a couple of times, but he's still in one piece."

"That's good. I wouldn't want Pluckenreck forcing you to take his place."

"Would you come after me if she did?"

"Of course, no matter how backward the TwenCen is." George drew me closer to him, close enough for me to feel his chest rise and fall with each breath. "But we can talk about that...later." He stroked my back in a way that meant he was interested in something else. So was I, but I needed a shower almost as much as I needed George.

We compromised; we showered together, so I could get clean and dirty at the same time.

Later, we huddled together on my narrow cot, and I told him not just what I'd shared with Pluckenreck, but about Sean's song and my breakdown afterward. Even remembering the experience brought tears to my eyes. I clutched George's hand for strength, then decided it was OK if I let the tears fall on his shoulder. I didn't weep as hard as I had before. Maybe I'd got the worst of it out of my system.

When I finished, George looked me in the eyes and said, "Sounds like the trip did you good. Did you warn Sean about his upcoming murder?"

It felt right to trust him. I nodded. "Not directly, but I sent a warning to his wife."

"What happens if he doesn't marry her?"

"Then he won't become involved in Filipino politics and get himself assassinated later."

"That makes sense." George sat up. "The physicists say this is a parallel universe, so there's no reason why the alternate history has to follow ours."

"Except to keep the wormhole open so the travelers can exploit this world."

For a moment, the only sounds came from the spaceship. I thought about the samplers I'd surrendered to the tech back on the base.

Would they send them to the lab, or keep them somewhere else on the ship?

"So, now your uncle gets to create his Sean Lyon clone." George eyed me as he spoke, as if afraid I'd do something.

I shook my head. "No, now I have to figure out how to keep him away from the child."

"Jo, you know I can't tamper with Sean's DNA sample." He hesitated. "You said Lizabeth told you how Professor Murakami distorted my work, right? If I'm implicated in another scandal like that, it would kill my career."

No; it wasn't fair to ask him to do that. And if I ever wanted to work in the genetics lab on the *Sagan*, I couldn't sabotage them myself. That left the motherhood option, but George wouldn't like it. I'd never asked him about kids, but he'd want his own. I braced myself for a lonely trip back home.

"There is a way I could reclaim that sample." I raised my chin to look at George. "If I volunteer to be the child's mother."

His eyes widened, and a half-laugh, half-gasp came out of his throat. For a moment, I considered ordering him out before he could reject me. Then I remembered how unpredictable Sean had been, and I decided to give George a chance, even though it would hurt more in the end.

"I—I never thought you'd want kids," he said after a couple of minutes.

I shrugged. "I don't know anything about them."

"Then what makes you think you'll be doing the child a favor?"

"You think I'd be worse than Uncle Jackass?"

"No, no." He laid his warm hand on mine. "It's wonderful of you to even consider the idea. I'm just saying you should think it through before you commit yourself to it."

Well, it wasn't an outright rejection, but he wasn't enthusiastic about it either. I wished I hadn't mentioned my plan at all. But it still seemed better than letting my uncle twist the poor kid.

"Whatever you decide to do," George said, "I'll be there with you."

He stared at me, mouth open as if he meant to say something else, then he shook his head and kissed me. I wondered what would happen when it was time for me to return to Earth, but for now, all I wanted to do was lie there in his arms and not worry about the next day.

* * *

The next morning, George and I returned to the genetics lab, and I regaled the other scientists with my adventures. Now that I'd completed my mission for the travelers, I was free to work full-time in the lab. "You could even start work on your dissertation, if you have a project in mind," Lizabeth said.

I grinned until I remembered this was a short-term assignment. "What do I do when I get back to Earth? Do you think you can recommend me to some other genetics lab?"

Lizabeth and George exchanged glances. "We'll see," she said finally.

I wondered what they were keeping from me, but I didn't have time to probe or fret about why they didn't want to give me the recommendation. I was due next door in the medical facilities to discuss the possibility of me becoming the surrogate mother for Sean's clone. Dr. Allnan ushered me into an exam area and drew the curtains so we could talk in private.

"I was sent here to collect a DNA sample from my famous ancestor," I told her. "When my uncle recruited me for this project, he asked me if I was interested in donating my eggs and/or hosting the pregnancy. I told him no, but—" I looked down at my fingers—"I've changed my mind."

"And you want to start right away, I take it?"

I nodded.

"We can do it here on the *Sagan*." Dr. Allnan set her handheld down to stare at me with dark eyes. "But you realize once the child is born, your uncle will expect you to turn it over to him?"

I bit down on my lip. That was the sticking point. "I never signed the agreement. We'll have to discuss it once we return to Earth."

She sighed. "I'm not a lawyer. Maybe it's best if I don't get involved in the legal issues. We should wait until we obtain permission from your uncle. Technically, he owns the DNA sample— "

"Oh, he does, does he?" My voice rose, and the doctor raised her eyebrows. I forced myself to take a couple of deep breaths to tame my anger. Rage wasn't going to help my cause, no matter how justified it was. "I'm also a member of the Lyon family, the one who obtained Sean's DNA. Yes, I got it for my uncle, but I haven't been paid yet. So until I see the credits, I figure I have some say about what's done with the sample."

She still didn't look convinced, so I smiled as naturally as I could. "Trust me, my uncle is very eager to start the process. He'll be even happier if I return with a child already on the way than if he has to wait another six months."

"It's not so much about making him happy as making sure he doesn't sue me."

I wanted to tell her not to worry; he'd take it out on me first, not her. I leaned forward. "Do doctors still swear to do no harm? Because if he gets to raise the clone, the boy will suffer a lot more than he would as my child." Assuming I could figure out the whole mother thing before I dropped the baby, or forgot him somewhere, or did something else equally stupid....

Dr. Allnan rose and inspected the medical supplies in the cabinet, but she didn't select any of them. After a few minutes of silence, she turned to me. "All right. I'm still not sure this will work out the way you think it will, but we'll try it."

I wanted to scream with joy and jump up and down like one of Sean's more ardent fans, but I didn't. Instead, I grinned as easily as if I did it all the time.

The doctor smiled at me for a moment before her face became serious again. "I should warn you, this won't be easy. Since you're young, I'm assuming your eggs are in prime condition and that your overall health is good, but I'll still have to test you first. If you pass, we'll induce superovulation with hormones, then harvest your eggs. We'll probably be able to create several viable embryos, but getting one—hopefully only one—to implant successfully is the hardest part."

I'd already reviewed this information before breakfast. "Might as well get started, then."

I spent the rest of the day in the sterile-smelling med lab, doing my best to lie still on the cold table while they scanned me with every medical instrument you can think of. Dr. Allnan returned after I got dressed. "It's a go. When was your last period?"

"About three weeks ago."

"Then we can start the hormone treatment with your next cycle."

I grinned. "Thank you, Dr. Allnan."

"You might not feel so thankful after two weeks of PMS and shots in the butt every day," she said wryly.

I was glad George wasn't around to hear that.

I returned to my cabin to rest and check my messages. To my surprise, there was another holo from Dad. My first instinct was to trash it. Even if it was something important, he could have one of his lawyers contact me. Then I remembered Sean hadn't been the enemy I'd thought he would be. Maybe it was time to stop treating my father like one too. For the first time in I don't remember how many years, I listened to one of his messages.

Dad's image appeared above my handheld. It'd been so long since I'd seen him that I was shocked by how weary he looked, with sunken-in eyes and iron-gray hair. He was too young to look that old; he was only in his forties. "Hi, Jo." Even his voice sounded defeated. "I know you might never listen to this, but I keep hoping someday you'll respond. If you're listening, I'm sorry I didn't do a better job of being your father." He hesitated. "You've probably heard by now we lost your mother. We couldn't stand each other in the end, but she was the first woman I ever loved. Even now, it still felt like I lost part of myself with her…." He sighed. "I just wanted to find out how you were holding up. You were always closer to her; I'm sure this isn't easy for you…."

I paused the holo. "It's about time you realized that, you…you…" For once, I didn't have the heart to call him names. He hadn't been the best dad in the world, but that was a problem generations in the making. Time for a Lyon—me—to step up and be a better parent. Maybe that meant I had to look backward to my dad instead of just forward to my soon-to-be-son. I resumed playing the holo.

"But if there's anything I can do for you, or if you just want to talk, message me. You know how to contact me if you want to. Maybe you don't, but as Grandpa said, the future starts now." He smiled ironically;

Sean had said that in one of his final interviews. Dad looked directly into the holorecorder. "Love, Dad. Ian Lyon out."

The holo ended. I stared at empty space for several moments before playing Sean's "Father, Farewell" song and thinking about his performance at the White Knight. I didn't cry this time, but my handheld trembled. I had to place it on my desk so I could record my own message. I stared at my handheld for a few minutes before I was able to reply. "Hi, Dad. Yeah, it's been a while, hasn't it?" I choked back a laugh. "I've got a lot to tell you."

I told him about George, my work on the *Sagan*, and my encounter with Great-Granddad. Then I paused the recording. Did I dare tell him about my plans to mother Sean's clone? If he told my uncle, he'd find some way to take the child. But Dad was the only person I knew with enough credits and clout to help me. Finally I took a risk and revealed my plan. "I know Uncle Jackass won't like this; he'll try to take the boy from me," I said at the end. "But he needs a chance to grow up normally. We know firsthand how hard it is to be Sean's descendants; let's not make this kid go through that. Dad, if you can manage a miracle and change Uncle Jackass's mind, or block him somehow, I'd really appreciate it." I took a deep breath. "I haven't been the best daughter either, Dad, but I still love you. Joanna Lyon out."

I sent it immediately, before I could change my mind.

CHAPTER NINE

I was glad I sent Dad my message before I started the hormone treatments. They were as bad as Dr. Allnan had said they'd be. The shots had to be given every twelve hours, and they made my back sore. I used pillows and wedges to keep me on my stomach at night. I gave up caffeine—one of the worst sacrifices I've ever made, and I bloated like a retired supermodel who'd just discovered chocolate. I could deal with all that, but my moods were out of control. One day in the lab when I discovered one of my cultures had been contaminated, tears gathered in my eyes. I refused to cry over something so trivial, even if it did throw off my experiment. I blinked hard, then threw the Petri dish into an autoclave bag with enough force to shatter the plastic.

"Just wait, George," Lizabeth said after she returned a tray of cultures to the incubator room. "You think she's bad now, wait until she's eight months pregnant. She'll get stuck between the benches, and she'll bawl like a baby!" She winked at me, but I didn't respond. By the time I was that far along, I'd be back on Earth, my trip a memory.

A look of alarm crossed George's face. "I hope we're stocked up on ice cream," he said. I wasn't sure if he was kidding or not.

"Screw both of you." I slammed the autoclave door. "You think it's so funny, Lizabeth, why don't you get pregnant?"

Her expression became serious. "Actually, Olivia and I have been talking about getting inseminated. If we're going to have kids, we should do it before we get too old. We can't decide which one of us should carry the baby."

"Why not both of you? Misery loves company."

"Maybe we'll do that," Lizabeth said.

"That'd be nice." It was too bad we wouldn't be able to keep in touch real-time.

The next morning, after Dr. Allnan finished examining me, she said, "Well, it looks like we're ready for the harvest. Feel up for it? It shouldn't be too bad. I'll give you a light sedative and local anesthesia, but you won't feel like working afterwards."

I notified Ferdie, who wished me luck. They sedated me and placed me in front of a scanner. I watched the monitor as a tech stuck a syringe in me. He delicately probed several follicles, popping them like balloons as he sucked out my eggs. "We got eight, Dr. Allnan," he said after he finished.

That was one of Sean's lucky numbers; I knew it was probably a coincidence, but I still hoped it was a good sign.

Ferdie kept me scrambling in the lab the next three days, and Dr. Allnan refused to tell me anything. When she finally summoned me, George came along to hear the news.

"One egg wasn't usable, and four of them didn't divide after we added the foreign DNA." She showed me the lab reports. "But the last three eggs are developing nicely. We even introduced some mitochondria from the samples, so the child will carry both yours and Sean's. If you're ready, we can inject the embryos into your uterus right now."

"Three of them?" I raised my eyebrows. "I don't want triplets! One Lyon is more than a handful as it is."

"That you are," George said. I stuck my tongue out at him, but he grinned.

"Odds are they won't all implant correctly," Dr. Allnan explained. "We do this to increase the chances of a successful pregnancy."

George and I looked at each other; it struck me there'd be no turning back after this point. "Well?" I asked him.

"It's not up to me; I'm not the one who's going to be pregnant for the next nine months. Are you sure you want this, Jo?"

I only hesitated for a few seconds. "Yeah. Let's do it."

The procedure was even easier than the egg harvest: a local anesthetic, a carefully aimed injection, and that was it. George held my hand as I lay still for half an hour afterwards. I put my hand protectively over my stomach as we left.

"Why don't we go somewhere private for dinner?" he asked.

"Sounds good." Someone could jostle me in the mess hall and dislodge an embryo. I told myself that was silly, but I had someone else to worry about now besides me.

George led me to a holoroom marked "Reserved." Inside was a simulation of a beach. Deep blue water lapped the beach on three sides, while the fourth side was a jungle complete with monkeys and brightly colored birds scampering among the tall trees. In the center of the beach stood a picnic table; steak and chocolate smells wafted from it.

I stepped forward, taking it all in. It was warm enough to make me wish I'd packed a bikini. The sand didn't crunch under my feet, but if I focused on the sights and sounds of the holo, it was a convincing illusion. "Did you program all this, George?"

His ears turned pink. "I wish I had. This is one of the preprogrammed holos."

"It's still lovely."

He offered me his arm, and we strolled around the beach. The view shifted as we moved. He finally led me back to the table and attempted to pull out a bench, but it was attached to the table. I slid in and looked up at him. He'd never done anything like this before. Either this was a distraction from all the medical tests and procedures I'd subjected myself to lately, or else something major was about to happen. I had a feeling it was the latter. Even so, I held my breath as George sank to his knees in front of me.

"Joanna." He looked up at me, eyes wide as if he'd forgotten what to say. He gulped as if he needed to recapture the words. "When I first met you back at the beginning of this trip, I thought you were the most beautiful woman I'd ever seen. And as I've gotten to know you, I've seen that you're just as beautiful inside as well. Will you do me the honor of becoming my wife?"

I sat there, speechless. I finally found my tongue. "But...but I might be pregnant."

I don't think he was expecting that answer; he looked at me as if I'd asked him what DNA stood for. "Um, I was there, Jo."

"But not in that way." I took his hands between mine. "It doesn't matter to you that it's not yours?"

"He'll be ours. We'll find some way to raise him—together." He lifted an eyebrow. "If you want me with you, that is."

I leaned forward and looked him in the eyes. "Oh, yes," I whispered.

He beamed for a moment, but then his smile faded.

"Something wrong?" I asked. I hoped he hadn't had a change of heart.

"It's just...I wasn't expecting to meet someone like you on this trip, and I don't have an engagement ring." He squeezed my hand. "I promise I'll find one as soon as we land on Earth."

I couldn't resist teasing him. "You planned all this, but you couldn't find a placeholder ring?"

"Like what?" He patted his pants pockets. "All I have on me is my handheld and some autoclave tape...."

He pulled the roll out of his pocket. The inner core would have fit around two of my fingers. He looked back and forth between the tape and my hand.

"Don't tell me you have an idea," I said.

"I won't do it if you think it's stupid."

"Just show me what you have in mind."

He tore off a piece of tape, folded it over itself to cover the adhesive, and played around with it until he molded it around my ring finger. I couldn't help staring at it.

George's mouth drooped. "You don't like it?"

It itched, but I resisted the urge to scratch my finger. "I love it. Just as long as you don't expect me to autoclave my hand."

"Let's see how heat-resistant it is," he said in a rough voice.

His kiss was hot, but dinner was cold by the time we got around to eating.

* * *

I was supposed to take it easy for the next ten days, but I still managed to stay busy. George and I planned to marry as soon as we returned to our own Earth. Trying to arrange details when we'd just passed through the wormhole was more complicated than visiting the TwenCen. Ferdie and I also discussed my future; he was so pleased about the way I'd handled the mission that he wanted to keep me in the lab. "This way, I make sure George sticks around too," he said. "A happy couple is more likely to stay in space than someone still looking for love."

Even a wedding, a dissertation, and a new job couldn't distract me from constantly wondering if I was pregnant. What if the procedure failed? I'd have to go through the whole damn process all over again, maybe several times. And if I wasn't pregnant by the time I returned to Earth, Uncle Jackass might refuse to give me any rights over the child.

Day eleven post-implantation, I returned to the medical lab as soon as Dr. Allnan was on duty. "Can I test yet?"

She smiled. "Yes, impatient one."

"Great." I looked around the exam room. "Where's a pregnancy test?"

She plugged a needle into her medical handheld. "I was planning to do a blood test since it'll be more sensitive, but if you want to pee in a cup like generations of other women, you can do that too."

I was over-prepared for the traditional test; it was hard to keep still enough for her to withdraw a few milliliters of blood. I rushed into the head and relieved myself into the specially coated cup. I forced myself not to look until I'd washed my hands. A giant red "P" had appeared on the bottom.

My hands trembled as I picked up the cup, then pushed the door open. Dr. Allnan had assured me the false positive rate for modern tests was virtually nil, but I wanted to make sure. But all the confirmation I needed showed in her grin.

"Congratulations, Joanna, you're pregnant." She held out her handheld to me, but I couldn't make out the results. "I can't normally say this so early in a pregnancy, but…it's a boy."

CHAPTER TEN

"Given any thought to a name yet?" George asked later that evening. We sat on my cot, glasses of non-alcoholic wine in our hands.

"No Sean or John names," I replied immediately. "I don't even want names that start with J or S. We have to treat this child as a unique person from the start." I looked sideways at my soon-to-be husband. "Though we could name him after you…"

He shook his head. "It'll be too confusing having two Georges around."

I was determined to honor my George in some way, though. "What's your middle name? You never told me."

"Paul."

I remembered one of the musicians who'd performed with Sean was named Paul. Sean had encountered other Pauls during his life, including two more musicians and a journalist, but the name was common enough not to have strong Sean associations. "Paul Harrison...Paul Lyon Harrison," I said, testing the name. It sounded good to me. With a name like that, Paul could be whomever he wanted to be, not my uncle's creature.

George nodded as if the matter was settled. "To Paul, then."

We toasted our very young son. George finished his wine first and set the glass aside, then faced me again. "So, when are you going to tell your uncle? And what will you say?"

I scowled, the sweet afternotes of the wine becoming harsh. "I'd rather not tell him anything until I have to. Why not just walk off the shuttle and show him my belly?"

George's voice sharpened slightly. "You know this is only half the battle, Jo. He could still sue you and the doctors if you don't turn over the DNA sequence—or even the child—to him."

"That's why I can't say anything now. It'll just give him more time to hire lawyers."

"Perhaps we'd better hire one of our own, then."

At least he was going to stick with me. I squeezed his hand. "When we get close enough to our Earth, I'll contact someone."

I didn't remind him I was a graduate student with more loans than lucre. I couldn't afford a law student, let alone someone clever enough to compete with Jackass's sharks. I had to find a way to bring Paul back onto the *Sagan* with me. If Jackass wanted my son, he'd have to travel across space to get him.

* * *

Between working on my dissertation—a project comparing how well a computer program to measure the genetic diversity of a species did against direct genetic tests—and coping with my pregnancy, the return trip to Earth felt much shorter than the outgoing one. Or perhaps it had something to do with my morning sickness during the first trimester. I ate crackers before getting out of bed; that helped, but it was still hard to muster an appetite. I went to bed early to counter the fatigue. I worked as hard as I could in the afternoons, though. I didn't want Ferdie to think I was lazy.

"Using the head again, Jo?" he asked one morning. "What's it going to be like when you're eight months along? Shall we just move your equipment in there, or will you let us use it too?"

By this point, I was in my middle trimester and past my morning sickness. I didn't think I was using the head more than anyone else. But before I could defend myself, Olivia looked up from the sequencer she was repairing. "Hey, Ferdie, did Lizabeth tell you both of us are going to get inseminated during layover?"

He paled. "Three pregnant women, in the same lab, at once? *Mein lieber Gott, nein!*" He rushed into his office and shut the door. Olivia and I looked at each other, then laughed.

I turned twenty-five a month before we were supposed to arrive on Earth. A message arrived from Dad while I was reviewing my data. He had shadows under his eyes, but his smile seemed warm. "Happy birthday, my daughter. I can't tell you how much it meant to me to hear from you. I can hardly wait to hear more about your visit with Sean—and this George guy. I still find it hard to believe you're going to be a mother when I keep picturing you as a little girl." He paused. "I've tried talking to Jack about his project, but he insists on going through with it." Another long pause. "We'll discuss it when you return. I'm pretty busy with something else. Looking forward to seeing you soon. Love, Ian Lyon."

I listened again, hoping I'd misheard. That was it? This was the most important thing I'd ever done, and he was too busy with some unnamed project to help me? I shouldn't have bothered contacting him. I rested my head on my arms, suddenly drained. I could be going through all of this for nothing.

George shook my shoulder. "Tired, hon? Or is something wrong?"

I played my dad's message for him. He looked at me as if he didn't understand. "Is he always this busy?"

"How would I know when I've barely spoken to him in the last seven years?" I shoved my handheld away. "He's letting me down—again."

"Maybe it's not as bad as you think. Maybe he's got his own plan and doesn't want to tell you in case someone intercepts the message."

That was so far-fetched I couldn't even smile.

"It'll be OK, Jo. I promise. Don't you have a doctor appointment?" He grinned. "Maybe we'll get to see an ultrasound this time."

I dragged myself next door, but Dr. Allnan seemed distracted. She only gave us a brief glimpse of our little blob before continuing her exam.

"The baby's fine," she said. "But I got a message from Golden Helix this morning. They weren't pleased we took the initiative from them, but they were very interested in our success. They want to meet with you when we return."

I felt Paul flutter inside me for the first time. I put my hand over him, marveling at the movement. *Don't worry, son,* I thought to him. *Mommy's going to make sure everything's going to be all right.*

Mommy never was a good liar.

CHAPTER ELEVEN

A new wardrobe of maternity clothes waited for me in our Chicago hotel room. I'd had to borrow surgical scrubs while I was on the *Sagan*, and I was so sick of them I wanted to burn them. "I can't wait to wear jeans again!" I said as I inspected them. The jeans were for the lab; I had ordered something more formal for the meeting with my old boss, World Music, and Uncle Jackass. I donned a pair of black maternity trousers, a black tunic, and a red blazer. I pulled my hair back from my face and secured it with a barrette. No more hiding who I was; let them see who they were dealing with.

George nodded approval as he looked me up and down. He wore a navy blue suit, neatly pressed, unlike the wrinkled lab coat I was used to seeing him wear. The only piece of clothing he was wearing that wasn't new was his DNA-patterned tie.

"There's just one thing missing." He pulled a small box out of his bag and gave it to me. "I hope you like it."

I knew what it was—my real engagement ring—but that didn't stop a thrill racing through me as I opened the box. A brilliant diamond, flanked by my birthstone emeralds, winked at me from a white gold setting. Simple, but it suited me. Plus it would last much longer than the tape ring George had given me.

"It's beautiful." I carefully worked it onto my finger and put my arms around him. "I wish we could stay here instead."

"So do I," he said, resting his head against mine. "But we can't hide forever. Better to settle this now before Paul is born and they can take him from us."

"No! I won't let them!"

"Hush," he said, stroking my hair. "It's going to be all right."

Too bad my mixed-up hormones didn't believe that.

We arrived early at Golden Helix. Zoë waited in the reception room. This time, she wore yellow and black instead of pink and blue, and a guitar case rested by her chair. "Jo!" she said as she stood up and hugged me. "My, how you've changed."

"Yeah, I'm huge."

"You think you're big now, just give yourself a couple of months." She released me, then examined my face. "And how was it meeting Sean?"

"Indescribable. I thought I knew him, but he constantly surprised me." I smiled. "But worth it all the same."

"You'll have to tell me every detail." She picked up the guitar case. "I hope this isn't presumptuous of me, but I thought you might be interested in this now."

I stared at it for several seconds. Even after playing with Sean, it still brought back bad memories. "I'm a geneticist, not a musician."

Some of her energy drained away. "I know you don't want to play professionally, but what about as a hobby?"

"We could play duets." George half-smiled, making it hard for me to resist him.

I put my hands in my pockets. "I can't take yours," I said to Zoë. "Don't you play yourself?"

"I used to, but after I got married and had kids, I never had the time. All it does these days is take up space. I had it tuned recently; it's still in excellent condition. It just needs someone to play it."

"Well, if you put it that way…I accept." She passed the case to me; it felt heavy—yet right—in my hands. "Thanks."

"Don't mention it."

George tried to take the guitar case from me, but I refused to let him carry it. Just because I was pregnant didn't mean I was handicapped. Besides, I knew I'd get a reaction out of my uncle if he saw me with a guitar.

He didn't disappoint me. My uncle, Guzman, and a couple of suits from World Music were already seated, studying their handhelds. Uncle Jackass looked up as I entered; a smug smile spread over his face. "Welcome back, Joanna. Looks like the trip did you some good. So, are you finally ready to sign with World Music?"

I set the guitar down. "Not in this universe or in any alternate one. I want to do research, not go on tour."

"You know how many other musicians out there would kill for what I offered you?"

"Why didn't you sponsor one of them? Or did you really think you could force me into the studio?"

"What's this about forcing you into the studio, Joanna?"

I'd heard that voice recently, but not live; it was my dad's. I turned my head and stared at him, not quite believing he was truly there. He must have come from his PR firm; he wore a gray suit, and he was wired with his handheld. His brown eyes were shadowed as he looked at me. I stared back. He hadn't told me he would be here. Whose side was he taking, mine or Uncle Jackass's?

"How are you, honey?" Dad asked quietly.

"Oh, Dad…" I used to think if I ever met my dad face-to-face, I'd curse him out. All the defiant speeches I'd rehearsed in my head now seemed petty. All I remembered was how good it had felt to reconnect with him after so many years.

As I turned toward Dad, Guzman cleared his throat. "If we're ready to get started…."

No time for hugs now. George, Dad, and I took seats across from the others. Catherine came in with refreshments; I reluctantly chose a glass of cranberry juice over coffee. The social niceties over, we got down to business.

Guzman spoke first, leaning forward and steepling his fingers. "Well, Jo, it's obvious that you were successful in retrieving the alternate Sean Lyon's DNA and that the doctors on board the *Sagan* were able to create a clone from the material. Congratulations. However, since you didn't agree to become a surrogate mother prior to the pregnancy, the ownership of the child is murky."

George squeezed my hand before I could spout some foul language at him. Even forcing myself to count to five didn't calm me. But I tried to keep my voice level as I said, "I didn't think you could own a child."

Guzman narrowed his eyes. "This is a clone."

"He's still a human being, subject to certain rights."

My dad cleared his throat. "Jack, isn't there DNA left over? Why not go ahead and have another woman bear a second Sean clone?"

I couldn't hide my frown. Sure, that solution would spare Paul from Jack's obsession, but then another innocent child would suffer instead. If that was Dad's idea of helping, he should have stayed at his PR firm.

As if that wasn't bad enough, the businesspeople from World Music nodded. "The more, the merrier, like the Elvii twins we had created last year," the man said. "Think what a draw we'd have if we had a group of Lyons!"

Probably not much; my cousins had tried making an album together, but they quit halfway through. Zoë shook her head as if she agreed with me. "No, it would never work." Her dangling earrings swung from side to side. "Sean had a dominant personality. His clones would never be able to work together; they wouldn't mesh properly."

"Perhaps we could train them to play different genres of music," the female suit said. "Or if they both grow up liking Sean's music, we can encourage a rivalry between them. There are a lot of possibilities here."

Zoë leaned over to comment to her, and George whispered to me, "Would you accept that, Jo?"

Before I could answer, Uncle Jackass stood, and everyone fell silent. "There's no need for that." He spoke slowly, as if each word had to fade away before he could pronounce the next one. "One clone of Sean is enough." As he smiled at me, ice formed in my stomach. "Hers."

Fear melted in the need to protect my so-vulnerable child. I crossed my arms over my enlarged belly. "You'll have to get through me first."

He stared at me for a moment, started to speak, then pressed his lips together. "As soon as the child is born—"

"I expect to be millions of miles from Earth."

Jackass's face grew red, but I played my trump card. "I had to find a new job anyway, so I joined the genetics lab on the *Sagan*, where my fiancé works."

Uncle Jackass raised his eyebrows. "You're going to take him into space! That's insane! It's not safe!"

"Neither is Earth, Uncle. If you don't believe me, ask my mother. Of course, you'll have to hire a psychic first…."

"Or I could just have you detained here." Some of the anger had left his voice, but I knew he was more dangerous now than before. "You do have my personal property, after all."

Dad's handheld suddenly sounded. "Excuse me," he said, getting up. "It'll only be a moment." He left the room, shutting the door behind him.

He couldn't stop taking business calls during the most important meeting of my life. I wished I hadn't bothered telling him about this.

The female suit leaned forward. "Is this your fiancé? Are both of you planning to raise the child?"

"Absolutely." George rested his hand over mine.

The two suits from World Music placed their handhelds next to each other and typed for several minutes. Everyone else in the room, including me, watched them. Finally, the woman looked up. "Well, we think the child should be raised in a nuclear family. If he has a stable, happy childhood, he'll be more likely to write upbeat songs, the kind that get good play on HitNet."

I wondered where they got that idea from, but if it meant I'd get to keep Paul, I wasn't going to argue.

Uncle Jackass shook his head. "If we take the child immediately after he's born, he'll never know the difference. With all my resources, I can give little Sean much more than you ever will, Jo. Don't you think that's best? And if you're going to practice science, a child would just be a distraction."

I resisted the temptation to tell him my son's real name. "I'm his mother; I'll do whatever's necessary to raise him." I glanced back at the door; it was still shut. Damn it, why did Dad have to get that call? Wasn't he here to support me?

Uncle Jackass looked smug. "I'm the head of the family; I have the controlling interest and the final say. I vote we continue with the original plans and let me raise Sean's clone."

Well, voting was better than threats, but it was one vote for me, one against. And my former boss got to cast the deciding vote. George tightened his grip on my hand.

Guzman cleared his throat. "As the representative of Golden Helix—"

I heard the door open. "Who represents Golden Helix?" my dad asked.

Annoyance crossed Guzman's face. "As the president of Golden Helix, I do, Mr. Lyon."

"But aren't you required to do what your stockholders tell you to do?"

"We normally don't seek input from the stockholders for day-to-day advice on how to run our projects; they don't need their Net connections slowed by such details. There aren't any stockholders or proxies present, anyway."

"Really?" Dad raised his eyebrows. "That's funny; I'm a stockholder. As a matter of fact, as of two minutes ago, I own nearly thirty-five percent of GH."

Uncle Jackass's face turned first red, then pale. He worked his jaw for several seconds before he managed to get out, "So that's why you're here, Ian. You're a filthy bastard, you know that?"

"You're not exactly a clean old man yourself, Jack. But frankly, this isn't my type of investment. I think it's more appropriate for someone with a science background…like, say, my daughter here." Dad removed a stylus from his handheld and scrawled a large signature across the screen. He tapped a few buttons. "There you go, Joanna. Congratulations twice over, for your wedding, and the baby, and a belated happy birthday, and…and happy everything."

My handheld chimed. I turned it towards George so we could look at it together. There it was, an account with nearly 40,000 shares of GH, all in my name. I checked the current stock market price and did a doubletake. I'd be able to buy a hell of a lot of diapers with those credits.

"Thirty-five percent isn't a controlling interest," Guzman said. He sounded like he was being strangled. Too bad he was right; strangling him sounded very tempting.

"I know that," Dad said. "That's why I had my firm send statements to the stockholders I couldn't persuade to sell. We were able to get some of them to send me proxies specifically for this issue. Altogether, Joanna and I have voting rights for fifty-five percent of GH stock." He winked at me. "So, Joanna, how are we voting?"

I took a deep breath and looked straight at Uncle Jackass. "I'm keeping Paul, of course."

"Paul? You're naming him Paul? Sean wouldn't approve!"

"How would you know? You never met him!"

We locked stares again. The only sound in the room was the faint hum from the air conditioner. I tried to outlast Uncle Jackass, but I couldn't. For a few milliseconds, there was something not right in those familiar eyes, a menace more frightening for coming from him. It came and went so quickly that I doubt anyone else caught it. But I did, and it made me squeeze George's hand. "It's all right," he whispered, a puzzled expression on his face. "You won."

I knew the war wasn't over.

Uncle Jackass sounded normal when he finally responded. "Maybe this is for the best in the long run. I still think you should stay on Earth with the child, Jo."

"But my new job and fiancé are on the *Sagan*."

"Then how am I supposed to see…Paul?" His mouth puckered as if he found my son's name distasteful.

"I'm sure Jo will let you see him whenever she returns to Earth," Dad said. "Right?"

"Sure." The *Sagan* only returned to Earth every twelve to fifteen months, so Jackass wouldn't have much influence. I felt it was wise to give him a peace offering, though. I pulled out a copy of the concert

I'd attended and slid it across the polished oak table. "In the meantime, here's something you'll like, Uncle Jack. It's Sean playing at the White Knight, a performance that never got recorded here."

He snatched the disc and tucked it inside his suit jacket, then rose. "Don't forget to message me about developments, Joanna." He stalked out of the room without saying another word.

The suits followed him. Zoë smiled and turned to me. "Congratulations, Jo. I like the name. Can I see baby Paul next year?"

"For personal or professional reasons?" I smiled back. "We'll be happy to have you."

After she left, Guzman shuffled toward me. "Ms. Lyon, about your stock..."

"Yeah?"

"You weren't planning to keep it, were you?"

"Hell, yeah." I got guilty pleasure out of seeing him wince. "And I'll be reading the annual report quite closely, I promise."

He left quickly. I wondered what he was going to tell people.

Only George, Dad, and I were left. "So, Joanna," Dad said, "like your present?"

I looked back at him. "I can't thank you enough for helping me keep Paul, Dad, but…" I stared again at my handheld, at the amount of money Dad had just given me. "I really could have used this in college."

His eyes widened. "I thought you wanted to do it all on your own."

"How could I, when we're too fucking rich for me to get financial aid? Didn't you care at all what I wanted to do with my life, Dad?"

"Jack said he was taking care of everything for you and Cassie…"

"Yeah, well, he took care of Mom, but not me. Guess he thought it unnatural for a Lyon to do something else besides sing. Why didn't you check on us yourself?"

"Did Cassie ever pass on my birthday or Christmas messages?"

"What messages?"

"The ones I sent you every year when you were still a child. I wasn't allowed to contact you directly, you see. That's why Jack was supposed to be the go-between."

I froze. "Mom never said anything…" I whispered. Why had she blocked him? Had she been vindictive, or had she done it with the best of intentions? There was more to my parents than I'd thought, more than I'd ever know now with one dead.

Dad sighed as he looked at me. "I should have made more of an effort to contact you once you turned eighteen, Joanna, but it seemed you'd never forgiven me for leaving your mother. I'm really sorry about everything."

I glanced away. "I guess it's my fault too. I never listened to your side of the story when you and Mom got divorced."

"Well, if we're both at fault…" Dad suddenly grasped my arm, making me look at him. Looking in my eyes, he sang the lines from Sean's song:

Can't you forgive me,

And never more roam?

He didn't sound as grieved as Sean had at the performance, but I had to dig my nails into my skin to keep from crying again. One look at my dad's face, and I flung myself into his arms for a hug. We stayed like that long enough for Paul to kick inside me.

Dad pulled away and looked down at my belly, eyes wide with delight. "I felt him! I felt my grandchild move!"

I grinned. "Yeah, he thinks I'm a punching bag." I hesitated. "Maybe I can forgive you, Dad, but I can't stay. I have to keep Paul and my uncle separated as much as possible."

He sighed. "That's probably wise. But I hate to lose you so soon after connecting with you again."

"If you message me, I'll answer. And we can visit when we return to Earth."

"Something to look forward to." Dad turned to George. "You take good care of my daughter and grandson when you're out there in space."

"Don't worry, sir." George's face was as solemn as a promise, but he winked at me before continuing, "Jo can take care of herself—as long as she's not wearing high heels."

"Sounds like there's a story behind that." Dad offered me his arm. "Why don't you two tell me about it over lunch?"

We left together for a long-overdue family reunion.

* * *

A few days later, the three of us made a trip to the TransAIDS Long-Term Care Facility where Mom had lived. We all brought our guitars; I also carried a yellow rose. Mom had been cremated to destroy the viruses in her body, but there was a special memorial for the TransAIDS patients on the grounds. The ashes of each victim were sealed in a compartment in a long, hollow wall, then they mortared a piece of black marble with the victim's name, date of birth, and date of death over the compartment. The compartment locations were available online, but we chose to walk the wall and study all the names. It took a lot longer to find Mom, but it felt appropriate.

Mom's compartment was in the middle of the wall, about chest level for me. I traced my fingers over the engraved lettering. It was still hard to believe that I'd never have tea with her again. Dad leaned his head against her compartment for a long time, as if he were communicating with her. The marble was slick when I touched it again.

After I laid my rose on the top of the wall, the three of us played Sean's song.

I don't know if Mom still exists, but I like to think if her soul still lives somewhere, she heard us.

* * *

And so that brings me up to today, the day George and I get married. When I started making this holo, I didn't realize I'd have so much to say. I'll have to edit this down before I let Paul see it; there's probably some things in here he doesn't need to know about his mom! One of these days I'll get around to it....

Lizabeth and Olivia helped me finish getting ready; now they're off getting dressed themselves, giving me a chance to make this last holo. They told me I look wonderful, but I think they're just being nice. I might not be as huge as a whale yet, but my belly's bigger than before.

I'm still a little scared about getting married and having a baby, but at least I'm not alone anymore. I've got George, the most wonderful man in the world, and after what we've already been through, I know we'll be able to handle marriage. I've got Dad and my new co-workers to turn to for advice. And this may sound odd, but I've got Great-Granddad on my side. None of this would have happened if I hadn't met his alternate. Thanks, Sean, and I hope you and Great-Grandma Baby are together and happy.

I'm trying to think of something to tell you, Paul, some words of wisdom to finish this off. They're hard to find, though. I hope now that you know the truth of who you are and where you came from, you're not angry with us for keeping it from you—for however long I managed it. I didn't want you to go through what I did when I was growing up. You'll always be compared to Sean, and there's nothing either of us can do about that. But no matter what my uncle wants, you don't have to do what he says. No matter what you do with your life, I'm sure you'll do it well.

And you'll be loved, Paul. No matter what happens, both George and I will always love you. I promise you that.

Dad's limo has pulled up, all decorated with streamers. It's time to go to the ceremony. But I just noticed something odd when I looked in the mirror, something so strange I have to record it.

Maybe it's the pregnancy, or more likely, the wedding outfit. But for once in my life, I don't look like Great-Granddad at all.

ABOUT THE AUTHOR

Sandra Ulbrich Almazan started reading at the age of three and only stops when absolutely required to. Although she hasn't been writing quite that long, she did compose a very simple play in German during middle school. Her science fiction novella *Move Over Ms. L.* (an early version of *Lyon's Legacy*) earned an Honorable Mention in the 2001 UPC Science Fiction Awards, and her short story "A Reptile at the Reunion" was published in the anthology *Firestorm of Dragons*. She is a founding member of BroadUniverse and a long-time member of the Online Writing Workshop for Fantasy, Science Fiction, and Horror. Her undergraduate degree is in molecular biology/English, and she has a Master of Technical and Scientific Communication degree. Her current day job is in the laboratory of an enzyme company; she's also been a technical writer and a part-time copyeditor for a local newspaper. Some of her other accomplishments are losing on *Jeopardy!* and taking a stuffed orca to three continents. She lives in the Chicago area with her husband, Eugene; and son, Alex. In her rare moments of free time, she enjoys crocheting, listening to classic rock (particularly the Beatles), and watching improv comedy.

Sandra can be found online at her website (sandraulbrichalmazan.com), blog (ulbrichalmazan.blogspot.com), and Twitter (@ulbrichalmazan).